HENRY and the Paper Route

By BEVERLY CLEARY

Illustrated by Louis Darling

A YEARLING BOOK

Published by
Dell Publishing
a division of
Bantam Doubleday Dell Publishing Group, Inc.
666 Fifth Avenue
New York, New York 10103

ISBN: 0-440-43298-7

Reprinted by arrangement with
William Morrow and Company, Inc.

Printed in the United States of America

May 1980

20 19 18 17

CW

Contents

CHAPTER ONE

Henry's Bargain

ONE Friday afternoon Henry Huggins sat on the front steps of his white house on Klickitat Street, with his dog Ribsy at his feet. He was busy trying to pick the cover off an old golf ball to see what was inside. It was not very interesting work, but it was keeping him busy until he could think of something better to do. What he really wanted, he decided, was to do something different; but how he wanted that something to be different, he did not know.

"Hi, Henry," a girl's voice called, as Henry picked away at the tough covering of the golf ball. It was Beatrice, or Beezus, as everyone called her. As usual, she was followed by her little sister Ramona, who was hopping and skipping along the sidewalk. When Ramona came to a tree, she stepped into its shadow and then jumped out suddenly.

"Hi, Beezus," Henry called hopefully. For a girl, Beezus was pretty good at thinking up interesting things to do. "What are you doing?" he asked, when the girls reached his house. He could see that Beezus had a ball of red yarn in her hands.

"Going to the store for Mother," answered Beezus, as her fingers worked at the yarn.

"I mean what's that in your hands?" Henry asked.

"I'm knitting on a spool," Beezus explained.

"You take a spool and drive four nails in one end, and you take some yarn and a crochet hook —like this. See?" Deftly she lifted loops of yarn over the nails in the spool to show Henry what she was doing.

"But what does it make?" Henry asked.

"A long piece of knitting." Beezus held up her work to show Henry a tail of knitted red yarn that came out of the hole in the center of the spool.

"But what's it good for?" Henry asked.

"I don't know," admitted Beezus, her fingers and the crochet hook flying. "But it's fun to do."

Ramona squeezed herself into the shadow of a telephone pole. Then she jumped out and looked quickly over her shoulder.

"What does she keep doing that for?" Henry asked curiously, as he picked off a large piece of the golf-ball cover. He was getting closer to the inside now.

"She's trying to get rid of her shadow," Beezus
explained. "I keep telling her she can't, but she
keeps trying anyway. Mother read her that
poem: 'I have a little shadow that goes in and out

with me, and what can be the use of him is more than I can see.' She decided she didn't want a shadow tagging around after her." Beezus turned to her sister. "Come on, Ramona. Mother said not to dawdle."

"Oh, for Pete's sake," muttered Henry, as the girls left. Knitting a long red tail that wasn't good for anything, and trying to get rid of a shadow— the dumb things girls did! They didn't make sense. Then he looked at the battered golf ball in his hands and the thought came to him that what he was doing didn't make much sense either. In disgust he tossed the golf ball onto the lawn.

Ribsy uncurled himself from the foot of the steps and got up to examine the golf ball. He picked it up in his teeth and trotted to the top of the driveway, where he dropped it and watched it roll down the slope to the sidewalk. Just before it rolled on into the street, he raced down and caught the ball in his mouth. Then he trotted back up the driveway and dropped the ball again.

Henry watched Ribsy play with the golf ball, and he decided that this afternoon everyone— even his dog—was busy doing something that made no sense at all. What he wanted to do was something that made sense, something impor- tant. Something like . . . something . . . Well, he couldn't think exactly what, but something *important*.

"Hi, there, Henry!" A folded newspaper landed with a thump on the grass in front of Henry.

"Oh, hi, Scooter," answered Henry, glad of an excuse to talk to someone, even if it was Scooter McCarthy.

Scooter was in the seventh grade at Glenwood School, while Henry was only in the fifth. Natur- ally, Scooter felt pretty superior when Henry was around. Henry looked at Scooter sitting on his bicycle, with one foot against the curb and his canvas bag of *Journals* over his shoulders. He thought it must be fun to ride down the street tossing papers to the right and to the left, and getting paid for it.

"Say, Henry," said Scooter. "Mr. Capper—he's in charge of all the *Journal* boys around here— he's looking for somebody to take a route. You don't happen to know anybody around here who would like to deliver papers, do you?"

"Sure," answered Henry eagerly. "Me." Talk about opportunity knocking! It was practically pounding on his door. A paper route was important, and Henry knew that delivering the *Journal* was exactly what he wanted to do. It made sense.

Scooter looked thoughtfully at Henry, who waited for him to scoff, the way he usually did at almost anything Henry said. But this time Scooter surprised Henry. He did not scoff. Instead, he said seriously, "No, I don't believe you could do it."

Henry would have felt better if Scooter had said, "You deliver papers? Ha! Big joke," or something like that. Then Henry would have known that Scooter was just talking. But to have Scooter say, "No, I don't believe you could do it. . . ." Well, Henry knew Scooter really meant it.

"What's wrong with me delivering papers?" Henry demanded. "I can throw just as good as you can."

"Well, for one thing, you're not old enough," Scooter explained. "You have to be eleven to have a paper route."

"I'm practically eleven," said Henry. "I have a birthday in a couple of months. Less than that, really. I *feel* eleven, and if you can deliver papers, I guess I could too."

"Yes, but you aren't eleven," Scooter pointed out, as he pulled another *Journal* out of his bag and pedaled on down the street.

Henry watched Scooter toss a *Journal*, with an

experienced flip of his wrist, onto the front steps of a house farther down the block. So Scooter really didn't think he could handle a paper route. And he wasn't just joking, either.

Henry began to think. He'd show Scooter; that's what he'd do. Maybe Scooter was older and did have a paper route, but he would catch up with him somehow. He'd go to Mr. Capper's house on Knott Street—the house with the horse-chestnut trees in front, where the boys had chestnut fights every fall—and he would ask Mr. Capper for the paper route. He would act so grown-up and so businesslike that Mr. Capper wouldn't think to ask his age, and even if he did, Henry could say he was practically eleven. After all, if Mr. Capper was asking around for a boy to deliver papers he must be pretty hard up for someone to work for him. Why, the job was as good as Henry's already. And with a paper route and a birthday, he would be as good as caught up with Scooter.

Then it occurred to Henry that Mr. Capper might have asked other paper boys besides Scooter if they knew someone who would like to deliver papers. It might be a good idea to go over to Mr. Capper's house as fast as he could, before some other boy beat him to it. Henry ran into the house and washed his hands as far up as the wrists. He ran a comb through his hair and pulled on his jacket, which he snatched off his bedpost. He was glad his mother was out shopping, so he did not have to stop and persuade her to let him have a paper route. He could do that after the route was his.

After removing the unbusinesslike raccoon tail from the handle bars, Henry wheeled his bicycle out of the garage and was coasting down the driveway when Ribsy suddenly appeared and started to follow him.

"Go home!" Henry ordered.

Ribsy sat down on the sidewalk. He thumped

his tail on the cement and looked hopefully at Henry.

"Good dog," said Henry, and started to pedal down Klickitat Street. Ribsy galloped after him.

Hearing Ribsy's license tag jingle, Henry looked over his shoulder. "I told you to go home," he said.

Ribsy looked hurt. He was used to following Henry wherever he went, and he could not understand why he could not go this time. Henry sighed. "I'm sorry, fellow," he said, and pedaled back to his house. There he got off his bicycle and led Ribsy, by his collar, up the front steps. "I'd like to take you with me, but this is important. I can't have a dog tagging along when I ask for a job." He shoved Ribsy through the front door and hurried down the steps. He did not look back, because he knew that Ribsy, his paws on the window sill, would be watching him.

Henry zipped up his jacket so it would look

neater, and ran his hand over his hair to make sure it was combed. A boy had to look his best when he asked for a job, even though he was practically sure the job was his—if he got there in time.

Henry practiced being grown-up as he pedaled toward Mr. Capper's house. He steered his bicycle with one hand and jingled the nickels and dimes in his pocket with the other hand. He sat up very straight to make himself look taller. He tried to think what to say to Mr. Capper.

"How do you do?" he said politely to a telephone pole. "I'm Henry Huggins. I heard you were looking for a paper boy." No, that wasn't quite right. He got off his bicycle to address a mailbox. "Good afternoon," he said. "My name is Henry Huggins. I understand you are looking for a boy to deliver papers." That was better.

Then Henry spoke to an imaginary bunch of boys. "Sorry," he said, in a brief and businesslike

way. "Can't play ball with you now. I have to start my route." Yes, that was what he would be saying after his visit to Mr. Capper. "My route," he said to himself again, and just speaking the words made him feel good.

As he rode through the business district, Henry glanced at his reflection in the windows of the Rose City Barber Shop and the Payless Drug Store and was pleased with what he saw. Business-like—that was Henry Huggins. Why, he probably

wouldn't even have to tell Mr. Capper why he
was calling. Mr. Capper would look at him, and
right away he would see that here was a boy who
could handle a paper route.

"Young man, do you want a job?" he would ask
Henry, as soon as he opened the door. Maybe
Mr. Capper would be so busy talking him into
taking the paper route that all Henry needed to
say would be, "Yes, sir, I'll be glad to take the job."
Already he could see himself pedaling down the
street, throwing papers to the right and to the
left with a perfect aim. He would never have to
get off his bicycle and poke around in someone's
shrubbery for a paper that had missed the porch.
Not Henry Huggins.

And the things he could buy with the money he
earned! Stamps for his collection. A flashlight. Two
flashlights—one for his bicycle and one to keep in
his room. He could even buy a real sleeping bag
that he had admired in the sporting-goods store.

Then he could ask his friend Robert to come over and spend the night, and sleep out in the back yard. It would be lots more fun to sleep in a real sleeping bag with a zipper, instead of some old blankets his mother pinned together with safety pins.

Just then Henry came to the rummage sale in the vacant lot. Now a rummage sale was something Henry knew all about, because his mother had helped with such a sale only last year. A lot of ladies who belonged to a club gathered up all the old junk they could find in their closets and basements and attics and garages, and had a couple of men with trucks haul it all to a vacant lot, where they spread it all out on boards set on sawhorses. They sold the junk—or rummage, as they called it—for very low prices, and used the money to buy a television set which they gave to a hospital.

Since Henry liked old junk, he had enjoyed his

mother's part in the rummage sale and had been sorry to see the old dishes and lamp shades and baby buggies hauled away to be sold. He had been especially sorry to see a pair of old laundry tubs taken away, because he was sure they would come in handy someday for something—he didn't quite know what. But his mother had said firmly that he could not keep old laundry tubs in his room or in the garage either, for that matter.

Naturally, even though Henry was in a hurry, he had to stop to see how all the junk in this vacant lot compared to his mother's collection of rummage. He leaned his bicycle against a telephone pole and joined the crowd.

Racks of old clothes hung in the corner of the lot under a couple of billboards. Nearby was the furniture department: old-fashioned iceboxes, chairs with three legs, sofas with the springs popping out. All sorts of odds and ends were heaped on the board tables. Henry decided it was pretty good junk. He paused in front of an old electric fan. There were lots of things a boy could do with an electric fan, especially if it worked. Just what, Henry could not decide at the moment, but he was sure there must be lots.

"How much is the fan?" Henry asked the lady behind the table.

"Twenty-five cents," was the answer.

The trouble was that Henry could not very well carry an old electric fan when he went to ask Mr. Capper for a job. It wouldn't look businesslike.

"If I pay for the fan now, could you hold it for me until I come back in about half an hour?" Henry asked.

"I'm sorry, but the sale ends at five-thirty," the lady told him. "A junk man will come and buy up everything that is left over."

"Oh." Henry was disappointed. Oh, well, a job

delivering papers was more important than an old electric fan. Besides, when he got his route, he could buy a new fan if he wanted one.

As Henry started to leave, he glanced into a carton and what he saw was a great surprise. Four kittens, one black and white, one gray with white

paws, and two yellow-and-white-striped, lay sleeping in a corner of the box. They looked tiny and helpless, poor little things. But there must be some mistake. Kittens were not junk.

"These kittens aren't for sale, are they?" Henry asked a lady who was standing nearby.

"Yes, they are," answered the lady cheerfully. "Fifteen cents apiece. They're very nice kittens. Their grandmother was a long-haired cat."

Henry did not like the idea at all. People shouldn't go around selling kittens for rummage, as if they were old teakettles or something. "If nobody buys them by five-thirty, will the junk man take them?" Henry asked anxiously. Henry was so upset about the kittens that he forgot he was in a hurry. For a minute he even forgot that he wanted a paper route.

"Oh, no," answered the lady. "I suppose someone will take them to the pound." She spoke as if kittens were not very important.

The black-and-white kitten stirred and blinked its gray eyes. Henry could not keep from touching the soft furry head. The kitten yawned and showed its tiny pink tongue. Then it climbed on top of the other three kittens, curled itself into a ball, and went to sleep again.

This was too much for Henry. "I don't think you should let them go to the pound," he said.

"I don't either," agreed the lady. "I'll tell you what I'll do. Since the sale is just about over, I'll mark them down for you from fifteen cents to five cents apiece."

A nickel for a kitten! That was a real bargain. Henry gently stroked the black-and-white kitten with one finger and thought it over. If he bought the four tiny kittens he would be saving them from the pound, and that was even more important than getting a bargain. Of course his mother wouldn't let him keep all of them, but it should be easy to find good homes for the others.

Then Henry remembered the paper route. He could not carry a box of kittens with him when he went to ask Mr. Capper for a job. That would be even less businesslike than carrying an electric fan. And nothing was going to keep him from getting that paper route, not even kittens.

"Well . . . no, I guess not," Henry said to the lady. "They're awfully nice kittens, though."

The black-and-white kitten snuggled deeper into the fur of the other three kittens. No, Henry told himself, I'm not going to do it. I'm not going to buy them even if they are only a nickel apiece. My route comes first.

A yellow kitten mewed in its sleep. "It's sort of squashed," Henry remarked to the lady, as he carefully pulled the little bundle of fur out from under the other kittens. Every minute made it more difficult for Henry to leave. Henry fingered the money in his pocket. Maybe he could leave the kittens someplace along the way and pick them up after he had talked to Mr. Capper. No, that wouldn't work. A dog might get them. They were too little to know how to climb trees. And yet there must be some way to save them.

Henry thought hard. His jacket! It was just the thing. It was roomy, it had a tight knitted band around the waist, and it was a cloth jacket, so air could get through it. He could tuck four tiny sleeping kittens inside, zip it up, and no one would know the difference.

"I'll take all four," said Henry, and quickly produced two dimes from his pocket. Gently he lifted the kittens, one by one, and slipped them inside his jacket. Then he pulled up the zipper. Maybe he looked a little plump around the middle, but no one would ever guess that he was hiding four kittens.

It was late, Henry realized, as he got on his bicycle and tried to ride without joggling his kittens. He had spent too much time at the rummage sale. When he reached the district manager's house he leaned his bicycle against the chestnut tree, ran his hand over his hair, stood up straight, and tried to feel eleven years old. All at once his mouth felt dry. "Good afternoon, Mr. Capper," he whispered to himself. "My name is Henry Hug-

gins." He walked up the steps and rang the doorbell. While he waited he could feel his heart
pounding.

The door opened and Henry found himself
facing, not Mr. Capper, but his daughter, who
was, Henry knew, practically grown-up. She went
to high school.

"Uh . . . is Mr. Capper home?" Henry managed to say to the girl. She was waving one hand
back and forth to dry her red nail polish.

"Just a minute," the girl answered. "Daddy!"
she called. "A boy wants to see you." She continued
to stand in the doorway, blowing on her red finger
tips and ignoring Henry as if he were too young to
bother about.

Henry stood up even straighter and in a moment
a tall, thin man with crinkly gray hair appeared.
He was wearing paint-spattered overalls and
wiping his hands on a smeary rag, which he then
stuffed into his hip pocket.

"Hello there," said Mr. Capper pleasantly. "What can I do for you?"

"Good afternoon," Henry recited, in what he hoped was a businesslike voice, while he tried to look eleven years old. "My name . . ." Henry stopped. He felt something move under his jacket. "My name . . ." he began again and stopped once more. A large police dog appeared from somewhere back of the house and joined Mr. Capper, who stood rubbing the dog's head and waiting for Henry to continue.

Henry eyed the dog. The dog eyed Henry. Henry's already dry mouth felt like old flannel. Again something moved under his jacket. "My name is Henry Huggins," he managed to say, and gulped. His name sounded peculiar when he said it aloud—almost as if it were someone else's name. For an instant Henry had a funny feeling that maybe he wasn't really Henry Huggins after all.

"How do you do?" answered Mr. Capper, by

now plainly puzzled as to what Henry's visit was all about.

"How do you do?" said Henry. No! That wasn't right. That wasn't what he meant to say. Now everything was all mixed up.

Mr. Capper's daughter giggled, and Henry felt his face grow hot. He did not feel businesslike at all. He unzipped his jacket a couple of inches. The dog stepped forward and sniffed at Henry. His ears perked up, giving him an alert look.

"Here, Major!" said Mr. Capper sharply.

Major barked. He looked eager and his teeth were long and white.

Henry's jacket began to move and then to heave. Henry no longer felt eleven years old. He did not even feel ten years old. He winced as a kitten dug its sharp little claws into his skin.

"R-ruf!" said Major.

Mr. Capper grabbed the dog by the collar and jerked him back. The kittens began to scramble around under Henry's jacket. Henry felt one of them climbing up the back of his T shirt. The pinpricks of its tiny claws made him squirm. He clasped his hands around his waist and tried to hold the other kittens down.

Mr. Capper looked amused and puzzled at the same time. Major strained at his collar. "What have you got inside your jacket, son?" Mr. Capper asked kindly.

"Uh . . ." said Henry, keeping one eye on the dog and at the same time reaching around and poking through his jacket at the kitten between his shoulder blades. Another kitten scrambled up the front of his T shirt, and before Henry could answer Mr. Capper, it poked its head out of Henry's jacket and announced its presence with a small mew. Mr. Capper grinned, and his daughter went off into a gale of giggles.

Hastily Henry stuffed the kitten back into his jacket, but the kitten promptly popped out again.

Henry stuffed it back and pulled the zipper all the way up. "Just some kittens I got at a rummage sale," he explained, as his jacket rose and fell.

Mr. Capper's daughter thought this was very, very funny. Henry did not see anything funny about it at all. The kittens grew more and more lively. Henry could not think what to say next, with that dog staring at him. He wished he could turn and run down the steps, but he knew he could not do that. Mr. Capper would want to know why he happened to be standing on the porch, with his jacket full of kittens.

"R-ruf!" said Major eagerly.

Quickly Henry decided the best thing to do, now that Mr. Capper knew what was making his jacket behave so strangely, was to ignore the kittens and the dog as best he could and end his visit quickly. "Mr. Capper, could I have that paper route?" he blurted, and instantly he was sorry.

That was not the way he had meant to ask for the job.

"Well, Henry, I'll tell you what you do," said Mr. Capper kindly, and for an instant Henry felt hopeful. "You wait until you are a year or two older, and then come back and talk to me about a paper route."

Still Henry could not give up. "I know I'm not very tall for my age, but I can ride a bike, and throw straight, and . . . things."

"There's more to a paper route than riding a bicycle and throwing papers," said Mr. Capper. "A boy has to be able to handle money and see that the papers are delivered on time in every kind of weather and left on the porch, or in the mailbox, or wherever the subscribers want them delivered. There is more to a paper route than most people know about."

"Ouch!" Henry could not help exclaiming, as he reached inside his jacket and unhooked a kitten's claws from his T shirt. "I mean, I'm sure I can do all those things, Mr. Capper."

"I'm sure you can too, in a year or two," said Mr. Capper.

His smile was friendly, but Henry knew he meant what he said. "Well . . . thank you just the same," said Henry uncertainly. He turned and started down the steps.

"Thank you for coming to see me," said Mr. Capper. "And don't forget what I said. Come back in a year or two."

"R-ruf!" said Major.

A year or two, thought Henry, as he walked down the steps. Didn't Mr. Capper realize that a year or two was practically forever?

Just before Mr. Capper shut the door, Henry heard his daughter exclaim, "Oh, Daddy, did you ever see anything so funny in your whole life? Can you imagine carrying kittens around inside a jacket? I thought I'd die laughing!"

How unbusinesslike can I get, anyway, Henry wondered, as he rode glumly toward home. Nothing ever turned out the way he planned. He started out to get a paper route, and what did he have instead? Kittens. Four little old kittens. That was what he had. And what, Henry began to wonder, would his mother say about his bringing home four kittens. And what would Ribsy do?

"Can't you be still a *minute?*" Henry asked a kitten that had climbed up his T shirt and poked its furry little head out under his chin.

Well, just the same, Henry decided, somehow he would manage to get a paper route and he wouldn't wait a year or two, either. He didn't know how he would do it, but his mind was made up.

CHAPTER TWO

Henry and the Premiums

WHEN Henry returned home with his jacketful of kittens, Ribsy, who was waiting on the front porch, came eagerly up to him and wagged his tail. Then, sensing something strange, the dog stopped, pricked up his ears, and sniffed suspiciously at Henry's jacket.

"It's all right, fellow," said Henry. "You just stay outside a few minutes while I get things straightened out." He knew he would not be allowed to keep all four kittens, but surely he could talk his mother and father into letting him keep one. He opened the front door and called, "Hi, Mom. Oh, hi there, Dad. I didn't know you were home yet. Guess what I've got?"

"I can't imagine," answered Mr. Huggins. "What is it this time?"

"Kittens," Henry announced, trying to sound as if he knew his mother and father would be delighted.

"Kittens!" exclaimed Mrs. Huggins. "Oh, Henry, not kittens!"

"They're nice kittens," Henry said reassuringly. He unzipped his jacket and produced a sample, the black-and-white kitten, which he set carefully on the rug. The kitten looked uncertainly around the room and gave a tiny mew. One by one, Henry produced its brothers and sisters and set them on the rug. He thought they looked cute, standing there with their little pointed tails sticking straight up like exclamation points.

Ribsy, who was standing on the porch with his front paws on the window sill, did not miss a move Henry made. He whimpered anxiously and scratched at the window with a paw.

"Quiet, Ribsy," Henry ordered.

Ribsy answered with a short, sharp bark that showed quite plainly he did not like what was going on.

For a minute neither of Henry's parents spoke. They just looked at the kittens, which were beginning to explore this strange new room. Then Mrs. Huggins said, "Henry, I don't know how you think up things like bringing home *four* kittens. It must be something you inherit from your father."

"He didn't get it from my side of the family," replied Mr. Huggins. "Nobody in my family ever brought home four kittens."

Ribsy barked furiously, ran back and forth in front of the window, and barked again, as if to say, "Let me in and I'll get rid of those undersized cats for you. Come on, let me in!" All the dogs in the neighborhood immediately took an interest in Ribsy's problem and began to bark with him.

"I said 'quiet'!" Henry shouted through the glass, plucking a kitten from the curtain at the same time.

"Ouch," exclaimed Mrs. Huggins, unhooking a tiny claw from her stockings. "There go my nylons."

Ribsy scratched at the glass and gave several short yelps, as if he were trying to tell Henry how much he needed to get inside and clear out those kittens.

"Quiet!" ordered all three Huggins at the same time.

"Well, anyhow, Dad," said Henry, and explained to his mother and father about finding the kittens at the rummage sale. He did not mention the paper route or how he had happened to be at the rummage sale. From the way his parents were looking at him, he could see that the kittens were going to be a problem, and one problem at a time was all he could handle.

"And so you can't take the kittens back where you got them," concluded Mr. Huggins, picking a kitten from his trouser leg.

"No," admitted Henry.

"But Henry," said Mrs. Huggins, "you can't keep four kittens."

"No," said Mr. Huggins. "You can't keep even one kitten. A dog is enough—too much sometimes, with his fleas and muddy paws. Besides, Ribsy would never stand for it. Tomorrow morning you take all four kittens down to the pet shop and give them to Mr. Pennycuff."

"Aw, Dad," protested Henry, who did not like the idea of his kittens' being sold to strangers. He looked at the four of them frisking around the room and sighed. If he could not keep them himself, he wanted to know that they had good homes. He would rather sell them to the neighbors—the nicest neighbors, of course.

"Can't I sell them around the neighborhood myself?" Henry asked.

"If you want to. Just so you get rid of them," said Mr. Huggins. "You know, there is just one thing wrong with kittens."

"What?" asked Henry.

"They grow up to be cats," answered Mr. Huggins with a grin.

Henry knew his father thought this was funny, but he did not. Of course kittens grew up to be cats. Puppies grew up to be dogs. Boys grew up to be policemen or pilots or something, but this took a long time.

Henry felt that he had one thing in his favor. He did not have to take the kittens to the pet shop until the next morning, and perhaps something would happen in the meantime to make his mother and father change their minds. Maybe Ribsy would make friends with the kittens, and then his mother and father would see how nice it would be to have a kitten around the house.

The way things turned out, Henry had a busy evening. The first thing to do, he decided, was to feed the kittens and get them out of the way before he fed Ribsy. Feeding them was easy enough, but getting them out of the way was not so easy. Henry put an old towel in a box beside the stove and lifted the kittens into it. They climbed right out and scattered over the kitchen floor.

"Hey, come back here," said Henry, while Ribsy, who had come around to the back of the house, barked and scratched at the back door. All the other dogs on Klickitat Street barked in sympathy.

"Quiet!" yelled Henry, out of the kitchen window.

Mrs. Huggins, who was trying to make gravy, stepped on a kitten. The kitten screeched, and

Mrs. Huggins was so startled that she dropped her spoon, spattering gravy on the linoleum. She did not need to wipe it up, though. The kittens took care of that.

"See how useful they are," Henry pointed out.

"I know there are only four kittens," said Mrs. Huggins, "but they seem like a dozen."

Ribsy barked. He told the whole neighborhood that he was hungry and neglected out there, all alone on the back porch.

"I'm coming, Ribsy," Henry called, as he scooped up the kittens and put them in the box once more. Because the box did not have a lid, he laid newspapers across the top. Maybe the kittens would go to sleep if it was dark inside the box. Then he hurriedly served Ribsy's dinner and opened the back door. After a good dinner Ribsy might feel more friendly toward the kittens.

Ribsy trotted in, his toenails clicking on the linoleum, and headed straight for his dish, where he began to gulp down his food. The newspaper over the box moved up and down. An exploring black paw appeared, followed by a black nose and a set of white whiskers. The black-and-white kitten popped out of the box and was followed by the rest of its brothers and sisters. They scampered across the floor, straight for Ribsy's dish, and acted as if Ribsy were not even there.

Ribsy was not going to let any kittens get away with his dinner. He growled deep in his throat and went right on eating. The kittens did not care to be growled at. They arched their backs, hissed, and puffed up their fur so that their tails changed from exclamation points to bottle brushes.

Anxious to avoid trouble, Henry snatched up the hissing, spitting kittens and tried to hang on to them. As they struggled to get free, their sharp little claws felt like needles through his T shirt. "Hey!" protested Henry, while Ribsy gulped his food without stopping to chew.

The black-and-white kitten leaped out over Henry's arms and skittered up to Ribsy. Ribsy growled. The kitten swatted Ribsy on the end of his nose.

Ribsy yelped in surprise and backed away. Then he began to growl as if he really meant it,

and lunged at the kitten. Henry managed to snatch it up while the other three kittens escaped from his arms and jumped to the floor.

Three kittens at once were too much for Ribsy. He barked furiously and tried to run in three directions at the same time.

"Ribsy!" yelled Henry, trying to rescue at least one more kitten.

"Dinner is ready!" Mrs. Huggins called out above the bedlam.

Henry dropped the black-and-white kitten. Grabbing Ribsy by the collar, he dragged him across the kitchen to the basement door and shoved him onto the top step of the basement stairs. "You be quiet, see?" he said sternly. "How am I going to get to keep a kitten if you act this way?" Before he closed the basement door, Henry snapped on the light so Ribsy would not have to sit in the dark. The house was quiet.

"Peace at last," said Mr. Huggins, as Henry sat down at the table.

Ribsy whimpered. Then he barked and finally he howled. His voice came through the floor beneath the Huggins' feet, loud and mournful. From the kitchen came the rattle of pans that were being explored by kittens.

Mr. and Mrs. Huggins were silent. Henry was silent too. Leave it to old Ribsy, he thought crossly. He's spoiling everything.

In the kitchen a milk bottle crashed into the sink. For a moment Ribsy was silent, and then he began to howl even more dismally. Long, quivering wails came up through the floor—wails that said Ribsy was the unhappiest dog in the whole world.

When the Huggins had almost finished their uncomfortable meal, the telephone rang. "Yes . . . oh, no, Mrs. Grumbie," Henry heard his mother say to the next-door neighbor. "No, Ribsy isn't sick. He just sounds that way."

"That does it," said Henry's father, when Mrs. Huggins had finished the conversation. "We can't have Ribsy bothering the neighbors. Let him out, Henry. That dog knows he has a corner of the living room that he's supposed to stay in when he's in the house. For once, he will have to mind."

"All right, Dad," said Henry doubtfully, and opened the basement door. Ribsy bounded up the steps and wagged his tail to show Henry he was willing to forgive him for shutting him in the basement.

"Down, boy," said Henry, "and in your corner." Henry knew it would be a good idea to get the kittens out from under his mother's feet while she washed the dishes, so he picked them out of the cupboards and off the draining board and carried them into the living room, where they promptly decided that Ribsy was something they should investigate. With a low growl, Ribsy rose to his feet.

"Ribsy, *in your corner*," ordered Mr. Huggins.

Ribsy slunk to his corner, where he settled himself with his nose on his paws and glared at the carefree kittens. Henry was kept busy plucking kittens from the curtains and trying to keep them away from Ribsy. Every time Ribsy started to get up, Henry ordered him back to his corner. It was plain to see that Ribsy was not going to allow any cats around his house.

I guess Ribsy is too old to get used to a kitten, thought Henry, but it was a good idea, even if it didn't work out. He was not sorry he had rescued the kittens, although they certainly had caused a lot of trouble. Now he would have to figure out some other way to convince Mr. Capper that he really was a good businessman.

The black-and-white kitten was especially lively that evening. One by one, the other three curled up and went to sleep; but the black one frisked across the rug in little sideways hops and sprang at Mr. Huggins' ankles.

"Shoo! Scat!" said Henry's father, who was trying to read the paper.

The kitten promptly climbed onto his lap and poked an inquiring nose under the newspaper.

Mr. Huggins unhooked the kitten's claws from his slacks and set it on the floor. It trotted over to look at Ribsy, who gazed hopefully at Henry, as if to say, "Aw, come on. Let me at him." When Henry looked sternly at him, Ribsy gave up. He kept a wary eye on the kitten, but he did not growl.

The kitten skittered past Ribsy, venturing closer this time, and returned to Henry's father. This time it climbed the arm of his chair and patted the edge of his newspaper with a playful paw.

"All right, Nosy," said Mr. Huggins, setting the kitten on the floor once more. "That's enough."

Nosy thought this was fun. He scampered over to Ribsy and patted the dog playfully on the nose with his paw, while Henry stood by ready to snatch him from Ribsy's jaws. Ribsy, however, merely glared at the kitten, which quickly lost interest. It climbed up the back of Mr. Huggins' chair and patted Mr. Huggins' ear. Then it jumped

down into Mr. Huggins' lap and gave a small mew, as if to say, "Here I am. Pay some attention to me."

"Oh, all right, Nosy," said Mr. Huggins. "I give up. Make yourself at home. You will, anyway." The kitten began to purr with a sound like a tiny engine. Then he began to knead Mr. Huggins' lap by moving his front paws up and down. After that he washed his face, his ears, his back, and each toe with great care.

The room seemed so peaceful that Henry was able to return to the problem of the paper route. But when he tried to think about the route he found himself thinking about kittens, and when he tried to think about getting rid of the kittens he thought about the paper route. It was very confusing. And then all of a sudden Henry was not confused any more. He knew exactly what he would do—he would combine the two! He would go around the neighborhood selling subscriptions to the *Journal*, and with each subscription he would offer one free kitten. He would think up a sales talk, like a Fuller Brush man. When he had made a list of people who wanted to take the *Journal* in order to get a kitten, he would take it to Mr. Capper. And Mr. Capper would be so pleased with Henry that he would give him the paper route!

"Mom, how do you say it when you buy something because you want to get something that comes with it?" Henry asked, because he could not think of the word he needed for his sales talk. "You know—like buying a box of Oatsies because you want to get a space gun."

Mrs. Huggins smiled. "Is *premium* the word you are trying to think of?"

"That's it. Thanks, Mom." Premium! Henry would offer the kittens as premiums with subscriptions to the *Journal*. He could hardly wait to get started. Phrases he had heard on television, phrases like "absolutely free of charge" and "without cost or obligation," buzzed through his head the rest of the evening.

The next morning Henry found a box the right size for carrying the kittens and then went into the kitchen to gather up his premiums, who preferred that room to any other. Ribsy's dish and the refrigerator were in the kitchen. Henry thought the kittens were pretty smart to understand that food was kept in the refrigerator.

"Thank goodness," remarked Mrs. Huggins, as Henry caught the last kitten and put it into the box.

Henry stuck a couple of old cellophane bread wrappers together with Scotch tape, tied them over the top of the box, and poked holes in the top. Now people could see what nice kittens he had to offer. With a notebook and pencil in the hip pocket of his jeans, he started out to solicit subscriptions to the *Journal* and to find homes for his premiums while Ribsy, protesting, was left at home.

Henry, who had often seen Scooter deliver the *Journal* on his block on Klickitat Street, knew which neighbors took the paper and which did not. He chose as his first prospect Mrs. Plummer, who lived two doors down the street.

"Good morning, Mrs. Plummer," Henry said,

in his most businesslike voice, when she opened the front door.

"Why, hello there, Henry," said Mrs. Plummer, dusting some flour from her hands. "How are you?"

"I'm fine," answered Henry. He stepped closer with his cellophane-covered box of kittens, and opened his mouth to start his sales talk.

"Goodness, Henry," said Mrs. Plummer, before Henry had a chance to say a word, "I hope you aren't going to try to give me a kitten. If there is one thing Mr. Plummer can't stand, it's a cat. And you know the trouble with kittens. They grow up to be cats."

"Uh . . . no." Embarrassed, Henry tried to give himself time to think. "I mean, yes, they grow up to be cats—what I really mean is, I wanted to ask you if you would like to take the *Journal*. The kittens . . . well, I was just sort of . . . I happened to be carrying them." Realizing this was no way to sell a newspaper, he added hastily, "The

Journal is a very good paper. My dad reads it every day."

"No, Henry," said Mrs. Plummer. "One paper is enough for us, and we have taken the *Oregonian* so long I'm sure Mr. Plummer couldn't drink his breakfast coffee without it."

"Well, thanks anyway," said Henry, feeling somewhat discouraged as he backed down the steps. On his way to the next house he had to stop and retie the cellophane over the top of the box. The exploring paw of Nosy had worked it loose.

The second time Henry rang a doorbell, he was determined to begin his sales talk before his customer could start talking and say the wrong thing. "Good morning," he said promptly to the lady who answered the door. "I have a special offer today. I am giving away absolutely free of charge one kitten with every new subscription to the *Journal*." There! He had got in "absolutely free of charge," just like a real salesman.

The lady smiled that annoying grown-up smile that showed she really thought Henry was funny, although she pretended not to. "I don't think I'd care for a kitten," she said. "Could I subscribe to the paper without taking a kitten?"

Henry had not foreseen anything like this. "Well . . . I guess so," he said, "but they are awfully nice kittens. They are playful and house-broken, most of the time, and . . ." Henry tried to think of some more of the kittens' good points, but the lady's look of amusement embarrassed him. "They are without cost or obligation," he said lamely.

"How much does the *Journal* cost?" the lady wanted to know.

Henry felt his ears turn red. He had been so busy thinking about his kittens that it had not occurred to him to find out the price of the paper. "I—I don't know," he stammered, "but if you wanted a kitten, I'm sure it would be a bargain."

"No, I don't want a kitten," the lady persisted, looking as if she were about to laugh. "But I might take the *Journal* if I knew how much it costs."

"I—I'll find out," stammered Henry, and turned to go. He felt pretty silly. I'm sure some salesman, he thought, not even knowing the price of the paper I'm trying to sell. The Fuller Brush man wouldn't be able to sell a toothbrush if he did not know how much to charge. Henry decided, for the time being, to give up asking people to subscribe to the *Journal* and just try to find homes for his kittens. He would ask twenty-five cents apiece.

Henry went up one side of the street and down the next, ringing doorbells and offering his kittens for sale. One lady was allergic to cats. Another had a dog that chased cats. A third just did not want a kitten. Henry lowered his price to fifteen cents.

At the next house Henry met a lady who owned a cat that had recently had five kittens. She said she would be glad to give Henry a kitten. At another house a boy said he had a pair of hamsters that he didn't think would be safe with a cat around. Henry lowered his price to ten cents and began to think about lunch.

At the next house a girl said she would take a yellow kitten, but when she asked her mother for ten cents she was told she could not have a kitten. Then Henry met a lady who said she and her husband went to the mountains almost every week end and no one would be home to feed the kitten while they were away. Henry, who was hungry, decided to give the kittens away.

At the next house Henry found the owner, whose name he knew was Mr. Pumphrey, cleaning out the garage. "Good morning. I have some very fine kittens," Henry said quickly. "I am giving them away absolutely free of charge to people who will give them good homes."

"That so?" remarked Mr. Pumphrey, putting down his broom.

He looks interested, thought Henry, and hurried on with his sales talk—if you could call it a sales talk when he was giving the kittens away. "The kittens are playful and housebroken most of the time and they could probably catch mice if you have any." Henry spoke rapidly. "I am giving them away without cost or obligation."

"Very interesting," said Mr. Pumphrey, leaning over to examine the kittens through the cellophane.

"Their grandmother was a long-haired cat," said Henry, sure that this time he had found a home for at least one kitten. His luck was beginning to change. After Mr. Pumphrey had selected his kitten, he would go home for lunch and then find homes for the other kittens that afternoon. Henry took the cellophane off the box and held up a sample kitten. "See how healthy it is."

Mr. Pumphrey smiled. Encouraged, Henry continued. "Its fur is nice and shiny. And clean, too.

All the kittens wash a lot." Now he was giving a real sales talk, as good as any Fuller Brush man.

"They do look clean and healthy," agreed Mr. Pumphrey, and Henry beamed. One kitten had a good home! Perhaps Mr. Pumphrey would like two kittens.

"Yes, they are mighty healthy kittens," said Mr. Pumphrey. "I know, because they are the kittens I gave to the rummage sale."

It took a moment for Mr. Pumphrey's words to sink in. "You gave . . ." Henry's smile faded and with it his hope for a good home for a kitten.

"Yes," said Mr. Pumphrey. "You see, we're moving to Walla Walla, Washington, so we had to get rid of the kittens. We're taking the mother cat with us and we felt that one cat was enough to travel with. You know the trouble with kittens—"

"Yes," said Henry quickly. He ought to know the trouble with kittens by now. Half a dozen people had told him.

"They grow up to be cats," said Mr. Pumphrey anyway. "But I'm glad you're finding good homes for them. We didn't have time to ask around, because we have so much packing to do and so much junk to clean out of the basement and the attic."

Henry managed a weak smile. "Well, thanks anyway," he said.

"Good luck," said Mr. Pumphrey heartily.

I guess that takes care of that, thought Henry. The whole thing was clear now. People did not want kittens. He was tired, hungry, and discouraged, and he could see that there was only one thing left for him to do. That was to take the kittens to the pet shop and hope that Mr. Pennycuff would take them. If he wouldn't . . . Well, Henry could not bring himself to think about that possibility. Mr. Pennycuff *had* to take them. Wearily Henry started down the street in the direction of the pet shop. He never wanted to ring another doorbell as long as he lived.

"Hi, there!" Scooter McCarthy called out as he stopped his bicycle at the curb beside Henry. "What's in the box?"

"Kittens," said Henry, and decided to make one more effort. "I'll give you a quarter if you'll give one of them a good home."

"No, thanks," said Scooter, and pedaled on down the street.

Henry was not disappointed, because he had not really expected Scooter to take a kitten. After all, Scooter did not need to earn a quarter. He had a paper route.

"Hello there, Henry," said Mr. Pennycuff, when Henry entered the pet shop. "A pound of horse meat for Ribsy?"

"Not today," said Henry, as he pulled the cellophane off the box. "I wondered if you could use some kittens."

Mr. Pennycuff examined the kittens one at a time, while Henry watched uneasily. "I'll take them, but I can't pay you for them," Mr. Penny-cuff said at last. "I don't have too much call for kittens, and I have the expense of feeding them until someone buys them."

"That's all right," said Henry quickly, before Mr. Pennycuff could change his mind.

Mr. Pennycuff set the kittens on the shredded newspaper in the front window and Henry stood watching them as they explored their temporary home. Nosy was the first to discover a post covered with a piece of carpet. He went to work sharpening his tiny claws.

"You won't let anybody take them who wouldn't give them good homes, will you?" Henry asked anxiously.

"Don't worry," said Mr. Pennycuff, with a re-assuring smile. "I always charge a dollar for a kit-ten, because I know that anyone who is willing to pay that much for a kitten will take good care of it."

"Well, thanks, Mr. Pennycuff," said Henry, petting Nosy for the last time. He hoped this kitten would find an especially good home, with someone who would keep him supplied with cream and catnip mice. And feeling as if a great load had been lifted from his shoulders, Henry ran home as fast as he could. When he got there he found his lunch waiting on the kitchen table.

Hungrily Henry bit into a tuna-fish sandwich, and as he sat chewing thoughtfully, he discovered the house seemed empty without the kittens. He especially missed Nosy. He almost expected the kitten to pounce on his ankles while he sat at the table.

Even Ribsy seemed to miss something. He sniffed around the kitchen and looked at Henry in an inquiring way. "You old dog," said Henry crossly. "Why couldn't you be nice to the kittens?"

Then Mr. Huggins came in from the back yard, and Henry confessed what he had done. "You know," said Mr. Huggins thoughtfully, "I miss that little black rascal. The house seems empty without him." Mr. Huggins reached into his pocket and pulled out his wallet. He opened it and took out a dollar bill.

"Dad!" exclaimed Henry, and grabbed the dollar bill. "But what will Mom say?"

"I don't know," admitted Mr. Huggins, "but while you were gone she did say that someday we might have mice."

"Boy, oh, boy!" said Henry, and gulped his milk. There was no time to waste. Somebody might be buying Nosy that very minute. "But what about Ribsy?" he took time to ask. "He won't like it."

"We'll just have to train him to stay away from Nosy," said Mr. Huggins. "It won't be easy, but we can do it in time." He pulled a handful of change out of his pocket and handed Henry a quarter. "And while you are at it," he said, "you'd better buy a catnip mouse."

Henry, who stood up on the pedals of his bicycle all the way to the pet shop, was panting when he arrived. Sure enough, there was Nosy, asleep in the window, and in a few minutes Henry was on his way home again with Nosy zipped safely inside his jacket and a catnip mouse in his pocket. He finally had a kitten of his own!

But there was one thing that worried Henry as he pedaled toward Klickitat Street. That was Ribsy. He had had things pretty much his own way around the Huggins' house for such a long time that it was going to be hard for him to get used to a new member of the family. Why, he might even be so upset he would run away. Dogs sometimes did things like that. Well, Henry couldn't let Ribsy do that. He made up his mind to be extra nice to him. He would give him bigger servings of meat, and scratch him behind the ears, and maybe he could persuade his mother to let Ribsy sleep on the foot of his bed instead of in the basement. Henry felt sorrier and sorrier for Ribsy. It was going to be tough, but he would just have to make the best of it.

By the time Henry reached home, he was not nearly as cheerful as he had been when he paid for Nosy. He parked his bicycle in the garage and walked up the back steps, where Ribsy was waiting. "Hi, old fellow." Henry spoke gently, and scratched Ribsy behind the left ear. Ribsy wagged his tail and followed Henry into the house. In the kitchen Henry unzipped his jacket and lifted Nosy out. "Steady, boy," he said to Ribsy. "Take it easy. Everything is going to be all right." Henry set Nosy on the floor, far enough from Ribsy so that he could snatch the kitten up before Ribsy reached him.

To Henry's surprise, Ribsy did not growl. Keeping his eye on Nosy, Henry petted Ribsy, just to make sure his dog did not feel neglected. Ribsy paid no attention. Instead, he gave a short, cheerful bark, wagged his tail, and trotted across the linoleum to Nosy, who had arched his back and puffed up his tail. While Henry watched, Ribsy sniffed at Nosy. The kitten stood his ground. Then, to Henry's amazement, Ribsy flopped down on

the floor beside Nosy and began to wash the kitten with his long pink tongue. And the funny part of it was, Nosy did not mind at all.

"Well, how do you like that?" exclaimed Henry, as Nosy's fur became more and more damp. "You *like* Nosy!"

Ribsy stopped licking long enough to look up at Henry and thump his tail on the floor. Then he went on washing his kitten.

CHAPTER THREE

Henry's Advertisements

THE more Henry thought about doing something important, the more he wanted a paper route of his own. Every afternoon after school he rode his bicycle slowly past Mr. Capper's garage on Knott Street, where the *Journal* truck dropped bundles of newspapers for about a dozen boys to deliver. He listened to the boys laughing and talking while they untied their bundles and counted and folded their papers. Henry wanted more than anything else to be one of those boys.

And then one Tuesday after school Scooter McCarthy stopped Henry by the bicycle rack and said, "Say, Huggins, I'd like to go for a swim at the Y. this afternoon, and I won't have time unless I get someone to fold papers for me. How about you?"

"You really mean it, Scooter?" asked Henry eagerly, even though he had been thinking of swimming at the Y. himself. "All your papers?"

"Sure," said Scooter, pulling the canvas bag with "Read the *Journal*" printed on it off the back fender of his bicycle, and handing it to Henry. "Just put them in the bag and leave them in Mr. Capper's garage, and I'll get there in time to deliver them."

That afternoon Henry was sure that this time he was getting closer to a paper route. Never had any paper boy done a better job of folding papers and sure enough, just as Henry had hoped, Mr. Capper noticed him. "What's happened to Scooter?" he asked.

Henry explained his arrangement with Scooter, and was a little disappointed when Mr. Capper did not say anything more. He did not stop hoping, however, and after that he folded papers for Scooter once a week while Scooter went swimming at the Y.M.C.A. One Tuesday, when Scooter was late, Mrs. McCarthy came in the car to deliver his papers. Henry made up his mind that when he had his own route he would never let his mother deliver papers—not the way his mother threw.

While folding Scooter's papers, Henry got to know the other *Journal* carriers. Of course he still was not one of the gang, but he was getting closer. "When I get a route of my own," he now had the courage to say, "I'm going to save up and buy a real sleeping bag," or "When I get my route I bet I can have all the papers delivered by five-thirty." He talked about getting a route at home, too, and to his friends at school.

One Tuesday morning, several weeks after Henry had been regularly folding papers on Scooter's swimming day, Scooter spoke to him at the bicycle rack before school. "Say, Huggins," he said, "how would you like to deliver my papers for me after school today?"

Henry looked at Scooter to see if he really meant it. Quite plainly he did. A chance to really deliver papers instead of just folding them and then watching the other boys start off on their routes! Here was his chance to impress Mr. Capper! But Henry did not want to appear too eager. "How come?" he asked casually, as he snapped his bicycle padlock.

"If I can get someone to take my route I can stay at the Y. and swim for two sessions instead of one," Scooter explained.

Henry pretended to think it over. "Yes, I guess I can find time," he agreed after a moment.

"Swell," said Scooter. "Here's my route book." He pulled a grubby notebook out of his pocket. "All the names and addresses of my subscribers are written down, besides stuff like where they want the paper delivered. Like some people want it on the porch and some want it on the driveway. You know—stuff like that."

"Oh, sure," said Henry, "I know." He flipped through the notebook and then stuffed it into his hip pocket.

"You have to get all the papers delivered by six o'clock," Scooter cautioned him. "If you don't, people will phone and complain, and that counts against me. If I don't get any complaints for a whole month, I get a couple of free movie tickets."

"I'll get them delivered," Henry promised. That day was a long one for Henry. Spelling, arithmetic, social studies—he thought they would never end.

Even recesses and lunch period seemed to drag. Every few minutes Henry put his hand on his hip pocket to make sure the precious route book was still there.

And then that afternoon, just before the last bell rang, Henry's teacher, Miss Pringle, put down her chalk and turned to the class. "Boys and girls, I have an announcement to make," she said.

Probably we're supposed to remind our mothers to come to P.T.A., thought Henry, wishing the last bell would hurry up and ring.

"Glenwood School is going to have a paper drive to raise money to buy a new curtain for the stage in the school auditorium," Miss Pringle continued. "A week from Saturday all the boys and girls are to bring bundles of newspapers and magazines to the playground. Members of the P.T.A. will be there to measure the bundles, and everyone who brings enough papers to make a stack thirty inches high will win a prize. And besides that, the room that brings in the most papers will win a prize. But remember—all the papers and magazines must be tied in bundles."

Robert, who sat across the aisle from Henry, promptly waved his hand. "What are the prizes?" he asked.

"Everyone who brings in a stack of papers thirty inches high will get to see a movie in the school auditorium." Miss Pringle paused as if she were about to say something very important. "The movie will be shown during school hours."

The whole class gasped at this news. A movie during school hours!

Robert waved his hand again. "If our room brought in more papers than any other room, what would we win?"

Miss Pringle smiled. "We would win six dollars to spend any way we pleased."

Everyone agreed that there were lots of things they could buy with six dollars. Miss Pringle suggested plants for the window sills. Someone else thought a big bowl of goldfish would be nice. One of the boys suggested a couple of extra baseballs, to use during recess, but the girls did not like this idea. Trying to decide what to do with the money if they won made the contest more interesting.

Henry hoped his room would win, but his next thought was that he did not want to go around ringing doorbells asking for old papers—not after ringing doorbells to get rid of kittens. Everyone in the neighborhood would remember him as the boy with the cellophane-covered box of kittens and even if they did not laugh at him, they would look as if they wanted to. Maybe tomorrow he could think of some way to get a lot of old papers. Today he was going to be too busy folding and delivering *Journals* to do anything about a paper drive.

When the last bell had finally rung and Henry had started home on his bicycle, his friend Robert caught up with him and rode along beside him.

"Going to work on the paper drive?" Robert asked.

"Not tonight. I haven't time. I'm taking Scooter's route," Henry said importantly.

"No kidding?" Robert sounded impressed.

"Yup," said Henry. "Maybe I can work on the paper drive tomorrow. I wish there was some way we could get a bunch of papers without going around ringing doorbells and asking."

"You could advertise," said Robert jokingly.

"Aw, that wouldn't work, and besides, it would cost a lot of money," answered Henry, taking Robert's suggestion half-seriously. He couldn't afford to have an advertisement printed in the classified section of the newspaper, but there ought to be some way . . . "Hey!" exclaimed Henry suddenly. "I know what!"

"What?" asked Robert.

"I'm going to advertise," exclaimed Henry.

"But you just said—" Robert began.

"Never mind," interrupted Henry. "You just

wait and see. Now I've got to hurry. See you later."
He stood up on the pedals of his bicycle and rode
home as fast as he could. After drinking a glass of
milk and sharing two wienies with Ribsy and

Nosy, he sat down at the typewriter, which was on
the desk in the living room. In a drawer he found
typing paper and carbon paper, which he stacked
carefully: first a sheet of white paper, then a sheet
of carbon paper, then another sheet of typing
paper, until he had used five sheets of typing paper

and four sheets of carbon paper. Then he rolled the stack into the typewriter.

Click, thump, click, click, ping! went the typewriter. Henry enjoyed the sound. It made him feel grown-up and businesslike. *Thump, click, click, click.* He could not type very fast, because he had to stop and hunt around for each letter. Henry finished what he was writing and stopped to look it over. It read:

wWanted? oLd mewspapers and nagazimes for the gLemwood SChool paper drive. i Will come and get them and tie them in bundels. pPhome hHenry hUggins. At. 7-4139.

Henry had known there would be some mistakes, but he had not expected so many. He mixed up "m's" and "n's" and he never could remember to hit the thing that made capital letters at the right time. However, anyone reading his advertisement could tell what he meant, and he was sure he could do better next time.

Briskly Henry thumped, clicked, and pinged. He glanced at the clock and realized he would have to hurry if he was going to finish typing a page of advertisements and get to Mr. Capper's garage in time to fold papers. By the time he reached the bottom of the paper, Henry had produced an advertisement with only four mistakes. He pulled the paper and the carbons out of the typewriter, slipped the carbons from between the sheets of white paper, found a pair of scissors, and hastily slashed through all five sheets of paper at once. When he had separated all his ads, he stuffed them into his pocket.

Ribsy started to follow Henry out of the front door, but Henry shoved him back. "You stay home," he ordered. "I can't have you getting into fights along the route."

This time, when he reached Mr. Capper's

garage, Henry did not feel like an outsider. "Hi,"
he said to the other boys in a brief and businesslike way, as he dropped his bicycle on the driveway and found the bundle of *Journals* with
Scooter's route number on it. "Hello, Mr. Capper.
I'm taking Scooter's route today so he can swim
two sessions at the Y." Henry quickly counted the
papers in the bundle to make sure it contained
fifty-three papers before he took a *Journal* from
the bundle, laid one of his advertisements on it,
and rolled it up.

"What's this?" asked Mr. Capper, looking down
over Henry's shoulder as Henry rolled an advertisement inside a second paper. He picked up one
of the slips of paper and read it.

Henry felt uncomfortable. His typing was not
very good, he knew, but he hoped Mr. Capper
would not laugh. Maybe his advertisement was
a silly idea after all. Maybe people would just look
at it and laugh.

Mr. Capper grinned and said, "Quite an advertising man, aren't you?"

The other boys looked at Henry's slips of paper.
"You mean you're going to put these in Scooter's
papers?" asked Joe, one of the eighth-grade carriers. "I'll bet he isn't going to like that!"

"But I'm delivering the papers," protested
Henry.

"Yeah, but it's Scooter's route," the older boy
pointed out.

"Well, now," said Mr. Capper. "I don't think
Scooter can say a word. If he's willing to let Henry
do his work for him, he shouldn't object to Henry's
putting ads in his papers."

"It probably won't work anyway," said Joe.

All at once Henry's hopes were dashed. Joe was

probably right. After all, he was in the eighth grade and knew about a lot of things. Probably people wouldn't bother with his ad. Or if they did take the trouble to read it, they would probably laugh at him, the way they laughed when he tried to find good homes for the kittens. That Henry Huggins, they would say. I wonder where he gets so many dumb ideas. Well, it was too late now. He couldn't take time to unroll the papers and remove the advertisements.

Quickly and neatly Henry packed the papers into the canvas bag and lifted it over his shoulders. The bag was heavier than he had expected and made it awkward for him to mount his bicycle, but Henry did not care. He was off to deliver a whole paper route all by himself!

"Good luck, Henry," called Mr. Capper, as Henry rode away.

Henry's answer was a grin thrown over his shoulder as his bicycle wobbled down the driveway. Mr. Capper, the district manager of the *Journal*, had wished him luck! Henry felt so good that he whacked at a tree with a rolled-up paper just to hear the noise.

On the way to Klickitat Street, the beginning of Scooter's route, Henry had to pass Beezus' house. Beezus and Ramona were out on the sidewalk, where Beezus was trying to teach her little sister to jump rope. Ramona swung the rope over her head as hard as she could and when it hit the sidewalk, she stepped carefully over it.

"No, no, Ramona," cried Beezus. "Jump! You're supposed to jump over it."

"Hi there," Henry called, as he sat up straight under his load of *Journals*.

"Henry!" squealed Beezus, "are you delivering *papers?*"

"Yup," answered Henry modestly. Out of the corner of his eye he could see Ramona staring at him with her mouth open, the jumping rope limp

in her hands. Henry supposed he did look pretty grown-up and important to someone her age. He hoped he would meet a lot of people he knew.

Delivering papers on Klickitat Street was easy, because Henry, who had often seen Scooter cover the route. was already familiar with the customers. He pulled a paper out of the bag and hurled it onto a lawn. Then he rode across the street and tossed a paper onto Mrs. Green's porch. Everyone knew Mrs. Green was particular about having the paper left on her porch, and Henry wasn't going to have Scooter getting any complaints. He zigzagged down the street, throwing papers to the right and to the left. This was the life!

As Henry delivered the papers, the canvas bag on his shoulders became lighter and lighter. So did his spirits. It was with special pleasure that he threw a paper onto the steps of Scooter's own house. Henry hoped that Scooter would be the one to pick it up and carry it into the house when he came home from the Y.

When Henry finished delivering the papers, it was a quarter to six and the street lights were coming on. Perhaps he had been a little slow, but he still had fifteen minutes to spare. Not bad. Not bad at all, he thought, as he pedaled happily home-ward. The canvas bag on his shoulders seemed wonderfully light, and Henry whistled through his teeth. This ought to show Mr. Capper who could deliver papers.

"Hi, Mom," said Henry, as he went into the kitchen. "Something sure smells good." He stooped to pet Nosy, who was sitting beside the refrigerator.

"It's time to get washed for dinner," answered Mrs. Huggins. "And by the way, Henry, a Mrs. Jones and a Mrs. Ostwald called and left their addresses. They said they had some papers for the Glenwood School paper drive."

"They did?" exclaimed Henry in astonishment. He had been thinking so hard about the paper route that he had completely forgotten about his advertisements. And now his typewritten slips were getting results, even if they did have some mistakes! Well, what do you know, thought Henry, as he considered this piece of good news.

Henry discovered that he was unusually hungry. "Dad, serve me an extra-thick hunk of meat loaf, please," he requested, as the family sat down to the table.

"Not *hunk*, Henry," corrected Mrs. Huggins. "*Slice*."

"O.K., *slice*," agreed Henry cheerfully. He had a feeling, now that he had actually delivered papers, that the day when he would have his own route was not far off. And his eleventh birthday was getting closer every day, too. In the meantime, there was the paper drive. From the way things looked, his advertisement was going to keep him busy.

And it did, too. That evening Henry received half a dozen telephone calls from people who had old papers and magazines they wanted hauled away. On the way to school the next morning, Henry tried to figure out how he could handle the old papers and magazines. The thing to do, he decided, was to borrow a wagon—his own had been given to a rummage sale long ago—and pile the papers in his garage. Then he could tie them in bundles later. Beezus and her sister Ramona had a wagon that he was sure he could borrow, and Beezus would probably be glad to help. After all, they were in the same room at school, and Beezus was a sensible girl.

Henry was parking his bicycle in the rack when Scooter arrived. "Hi," said Henry. "I got your papers delivered O.K."

"What's the big idea, anyway?" demanded Scooter. "Putting those crummy ads in *my* papers?"

"But *I* was delivering the papers," protested Henry.

"But it's my route." Scooter raised his voice.

"But Mr. Capper said I could," Henry pointed out, certain that he was right, but at the same time not wanting Scooter to be angry with him.

"I don't care what Mr. Capper said," yelled Scooter. "It was cheating, that's what it was!"

By now the boys and girls on the school grounds were beginning to take enough interest in the argument to gather around the bicycle racks to listen.

"It was not cheating!" said Henry heatedly. Scooter couldn't call him a cheater. "You didn't want to deliver your papers last night, and Mr. Capper said it was all right for me to put the ad in. If you had delivered the papers you could have put the ad in yourself—if you had thought of it!"

The suggestion that he might not have thought of advertising made Scooter even more angry. "Ha!" he scoffed. "Anyway, it was a dumb ad and I bet it won't work."

"It will too work." Henry could not resist bragging. "It worked already. Eight people have phoned, and I bet a whole bunch more call today!" There! That ought to settle Scooter.

It didn't. It only made Scooter madder. "All right for you, Henry Huggins!" he shouted. "You don't need to hang around my paper route any more, wanting to fold papers!"

This stopped Henry. To have Scooter come right out and accuse him of hanging around startled him. *Hanging around!* He did not like the sound of the words at all. "Don't worry," he said hotly. "I wouldn't fold your old papers for a million dollars!"

"Not much you wouldn't!" retorted Scooter.

"And you can find somebody else to do your work for you!" answered Henry.

"I think Henry's right," someone said.

"I don't," said someone else. "I think Scooter is right."

Suddenly everyone was arguing with everyone else. Beezus pushed her way through the crowd. "Scooter McCarthy!" she said fiercely. "I think you're mean! Just because you were too lazy to deliver your own papers, you have to go and

pick on Henry. You ought to thank him, that's what!"

Henry's feelings were mixed. He was glad to have support from Beezus, and at the same time he wished she would keep out of the quarrel. He did not want the whole school teasing him about a girl.

"So there!" said Beezus, and stamped her foot at Scooter.

Plainly Scooter did not like being picked on by a girl. "Just the same," he said, "Henry better—" The bell rang, and Scooter stopped. The crowd broke up and the boys and girls began to make their way into the school building.

"Just the same," muttered Henry, "we'll see whose room wins the old paper drive." He was not sure whether Scooter had heard him or not, but he hoped he had.

"Beezus likes Henry," someone chanted. "Beezus likes Henry!"

Hanging around. The unpleasant sound of the words still rang in Henry's ears. They made him feel like someone who was in the way, a nuisance. That was the last thing he wanted to be. He only wanted a chance to show Mr. Capper that he was a good businessman. Well, that chance was gone now. Even if Scooter got over being mad, Henry knew that he would never go back to Mr. Capper's garage again.

Aw, I didn't want an old route anyway, Henry tried to persuade himself. But he could not make himself believe it.

CHAPTER FOUR

The Paper Drive

IMMEDIATELY after school Henry and Beezus, who was eager to lend the wagon and help collect papers, hurried to the Huggins' house, where they stopped long enough to tell Mrs. Huggins what they were going to do and to pick up some more addresses of people who had telephoned in answer to the advertisement. Accompanied by Ribsy and Nosy, who was a brave kitten when Ribsy went along to protect him, they continued to Beezus' house, where they ate some bread and cheese and drank some milk before they went out the back door to get the wagon out of the garage.

Beezus' little sister Ramona was hopping around on the grass. Pinned to the seat of her coveralls was one end of a piece of old jumping rope. "I'm a monkey," she announced, as Beezus pulled the red wagon out of the garage. "That's my wagon," she said.

"I know," answered Beezus, "but we are going to borrow it."

"No," said Ramona. "I need it."

"Oh, Ramona, don't be silly," said Beezus impatiently. "We'll bring it back."

"No!" screamed Ramona. "I need it *now!*"

Mrs. Quimby came out on the back porch. "Girls! What is the trouble?" she asked.

"We want to use the wagon to get some papers, and now Ramona says she wants it," Beezus told her mother.

"It's my wagon," insisted Ramona.

"Why don't you take Ramona with you?" suggested Mrs. Quimby. "Then I'm sure she'll let you use the wagon, won't you, Ramona?"

"Yes," agreed Ramona happily, because she always liked to be included in whatever the older boys and girls were doing.

"Oh, Mother," protested Beezus. "She'll just get in the way."

"But it is her wagon, too," Mrs. Quimby reminded Beezus.

"All right, Ramona," said Beezus crossly. "Come on. Let me unpin your tail."

"I'm a monkey, and I can't take off my tail," said

Ramona, as she bounced down the driveway with her tail dragging on the cement.

Henry wished he could think of some other way to get hold of a wagon. He was embarrassed to be seen on the street with Ramona and her jumping-rope tail.

"Let her go ahead of us, and just pretend you don't know her," advised Beezus. "That's what I do."

"I want to pull my wagon," said Ramona, bouncing back to Beezus and Henry.

"All right," agreed Beezus, giving her sister the wagon handle. "Turn at the next corner. We're going to the Ostwalds'."

When they turned the corner they saw a moving van backed up to a house. The painted letters on the side of the van read: "Tucker's Motor Transit. Let Tucker Take It."

"Hey!" exclaimed Henry. "The Pumphreys must be moving today. Their cat is Nosy's mother."

"I know somebody who has a seven-toed cat," said Beezus.

Ramona stood beside the truck, watching two men in white coveralls carry a set of bedsprings out of the house and push them up a plank into the moving van. "Hello," she said, twitching her jumping-rope tail. It was easy to see that she wanted the movers to notice her tail. There was never anything shy about Ramona.

"Why, hello there," said one of the men, grinning at Ramona. "What's this?"

"Looks to me like a little girl with a tail like a monkey," remarked the other man, and Ramona beamed with pleasure.

"Come on, Ramona," said Beezus. "We've got a lot of papers to pick up."

"Yes, come on," said Henry impatiently. The list in his pocket was a long one.

"I want to watch," said Ramona flatly without moving.

"O.K., you watch," agreed Henry, "and we'll take the wagon and pick up the papers."

This strategy did not work. "It's *my* wagon," said Ramona. She did, however, let go of the

handle in order to walk up the plank to explore the inside of the moving van.

Henry was tempted to grab the wagon and run. It had occurred to him that his advertisement might have been too successful. Picking up a lot of papers and magazines with a little wagon would not be easy. "Hi, Mr. Pumphrey," Henry said to the owner of the furniture, who came out of the house with a lamp in his hands.

"Ramona, come out of that van this instant!" ordered Beezus. "You're in the way."

"I don't want to come out," answered Ramona. "I want to see what's in here."

"You'd better run along," one of the movers said. "You might get hurt."

"No, I won't," said Ramona, as she stood on tiptoe and tried to peep into a barrel.

"Come on, Ramona," pleaded Beezus, but Ramona ignored her.

"Say, Mr. Pumphrey," one of the movers called from inside the van, where he was stacking the bedsprings, "how would you like a little girl with a tail like a monkey to take with you to Walla Walla, Washington?"

Ramona stopped trying to peer into the barrel

and smiled at the man who was paying her so much attention.

Henry saw Mr. Pumphrey wink as he said, "Sure. Know where I can find one?"

"It just happens that I have a little girl with a tail like a monkey right here," answered the mover.

"How much do you want for her?" asked Mr. Pumphrey, going along with the joke.

"You don't often see a little girl with a tail like a monkey," the moving man remarked, as he walked down the plank and up the Pumphreys' steps, "especially in this part of the country."

"I know it," said Mr. Pumphrey, "and I understand they're even scarcer in Walla Walla."

"I'll tell you what I'll do," said the moving man. "This little girl with a tail is in pretty good condition, so I'll let you have her for a nickel. How would that be?"

"It's a bargain," agreed Mr. Pumphrey, reaching into his pocket and pulling out a handful of change.

Ramona watched with big eyes while he selected a nickel and handed it to the mover.

"You're getting a good buy," said the man, as he put the coin in his pocket. "She has an extra-long tail."

At that Ramona ran out of the moving van and down the plank, grabbed the handle of her wagon, and began to run toward home as fast as her legs would carry her.

"Ramona, wait!" Beezus called, but Ramona only ran faster. The handle of her jumping-rope tail clattered and her feet pounded on the sidewalk as fast as she could make them go.

Well, there goes our wagon, thought Henry. Now what am I going to do?

"Come on, Henry," said Beezus. "We'll have to go get her. She thought they meant it."

"Hey, Ramona, come back here!" called Henry in a disgusted tone of voice, as he joined Beezus in running after her sister. Leave it to Ramona to spoil his plans! Now how was he going to collect all those papers, without a wagon?

With the wagon rattling after her, Ramona turned the corner and was halfway down the block before Henry and Beezus caught up with her. Beezus grabbed her sister by the arm. "Ramona, wait," she said. "It's all right. The men were only joking."

"No!" screamed Ramona, jerking away from Beezus. "I don't want to go to—to that place!"

"But Ramona," pleaded Beezus, "he was just pretending. He did it to get you to come out of the moving van." Then she added crossly, "If you had come out when I told you to, it wouldn't have happened."

"Say, Ramona," said Henry in desperation, "how about letting me take the wagon while you go on home with Beezus?" He had to get those papers, or the people who had answered his advertisement would be annoyed.

Ramona stopped in her tracks. "No," she said, with a scowl. "It's my wagon."

Henry was disgusted with himself. He should have known better than to have anything to do with Ramona at a time like this. But the trouble was, he couldn't think of any other way to move all those papers and magazines. He did not know anyone else in the neighborhood who owned a wagon, and his father had driven the car to work that morning, so his mother could not haul the bundles for him. He thought of using a wheelbarrow, but he was not sure he could lift a wheelbarrow filled with heavy magazines. Maybe if he took one handle and Beezus took the other . . . But they would have to get rid of Ramona first, and that would not be easy.

Henry scowled at Ramona, who had climbed into her wagon. "Pull me," she ordered.

"Oh, all right," said Beezus crossly.

As Henry looked at Ramona sitting in her

wagon, with her tail hanging over the edge, a thought came to him. He wondered why it had not come to him before. There was a chance it might work, too, he decided. You never could tell about Ramona.

"Say, Ramona," Henry began, "why don't you take off your tail?"

Ramona scowled. The surest way to make her want to wear her tail was for someone to ask her to take it off.

"Mr. Pumphrey said he wanted a girl with a tail like a monkey to take to Walla Walla, Washington," Henry pointed out. "He didn't say anything about a *plain* girl."

As Ramona stopped scowling and looked thoughtful, Beezus flashed a hopeful smile at Henry. This might work.

"That's right, Ramona," agreed Beezus. "Mr. Pumphrey didn't say anything about a plain girl.

He wanted a girl with a tail, because you don't often see one. He said so himself."

Ramona put her hand on her tail, as if she were thinking it over.

"Without your tail, he probably wouldn't even know you," added Henry.

"Of course ·he wouldn't," said Beezus firmly. "He would think you were somebody else, an ordinary girl."

"Yes," agreed Henry, "and there are plenty of *those* around. He probably wouldn't even take you to Walla Walla if you wanted to go. Not even if you begged him."

That did it. Ramona climbed out of the wagon and backed up to Beezus. "Unpin me," she requested, and Beezus unpinned the piece of jumping rope and put it into her pocket.

The wagon was Henry's to use at last! Now they could really go to work, and about time, too. Henry could not help feeling pleased with himself. That was the way to handle Ramona—outwit her.

"Say, Beezus," said Henry suddenly, when they were finally headed for the Ostwalds' house and their first load of papers, "somebody will be moving into the Pumphreys' house before long. I hope there is a boy about my age." He felt that a new boy would be especially welcome now that Scooter was mad at him.

"I hope there is a girl," said Beezus, "a girl who doesn't have a little sister."

Mrs. Ostwald not only had piles of the *Journal* and the *Shopping News,* Henry found when they called on her; she also had piles of *Life.* Henry and Beezus had to make four trips with the wagon to remove all the papers and magazines from Mrs. Ostwald's basement. It was hard work, because *Life* was slippery as well as heavy. No matter how carefully they piled it on the wagon, it slipped and slid and slithered. Henry was in such a hurry that

he threw the papers and magazines into his garage. He would stack and tie them later.

The second lady had old newspapers and *The Saturday Evening Post,* which was not as heavy as *Life,* but still pretty heavy. It was more slippery, though. The papers were dusty, and printer's ink rubbed off on their hands. Henry felt hot and dirty by the time he and Beezus had finished dumping the second lady's papers into his garage.

"Goodness, Henry, just look at you!" exclaimed Mrs. Huggins, when he went into the house. "You'll have to take a bath and put on a clean shirt before dinner."

"Sure, Mom," answered Henry. "Any calls for me?"

"Yes, several," said Mrs. Huggins. "The addresses are on the pad by the telephone."

At dinner Henry told his father about the success of his advertisements. Mr. Huggins laughed and said what Henry had hoped he would say. He said that after dinner he would take the car and help Henry pick up some papers.

Henry and his father worked hard that evening. It seemed as if all the neighbors had been collecting old papers and magazines for months. Some people gave them big piles of heavy magazines, like *Life* and *House Beautiful*. Others gave them small stacks of lightweight magazines, like *Reader's Digest*. Some people gave them magazines of all sizes, that were hard to stack. Henry decided he liked best the people who gave them *National Geographic*, because it was thick, an easy size to handle, and did not slip and slide. Henry and his father took everything that was given to them and tossed it into the Huggins' garage. Mr. Huggins said he would leave the car in the driveway that night. Mrs. Huggins said Henry had to take another bath.

Henry and Beezus, who had been joined by Robert, worked hard every day after school and on Saturday. They were slowed down somewhat by Ramona, who still insisted on going along with her wagon. Instead of a tail, she now wore a pair of her mother's old high-heeled shoes over her sandals so that she made clonking noises when she walked. Ribsy and Nosy romped along too. Wagonload after wagonload of papers and magazines went into the Huggins' garage. When the garage was knee-deep in paper, the children dumped their

loads on the driveway. Each evening Mr. Huggins had to park his car closer to the street.

Once Mr. Capper, who was driving down the street, stopped his old convertible by the curb, and asked, "How's the advertising man?"

"Fine," answered Henry, turning red to the tips of his ears. He did not feel that he looked business-like at all, with a dog and a kitten romping beside

him and Ramona clonking along in her mother's
high-heeled shoes.

One night Henry was awakened by gusts of
rain blowing against the house. My papers! he
thought. They'll be sopping. Then he went back
to sleep. By morning the rain had subsided to a
drizzle, and when Henry rushed out to inspect his
papers, the whole world seemed soggy. The lawn

was soggy, the leaves in the gutter were soggy, and the newspapers on top of his heap were soggiest of all.

"Henry," said Mr. Huggins at breakfast, "hadn't you better stop collecting papers and start tying them up? You're going to have quite a job getting them all made up into bundles. And you still have to get them to school, you know."

When the last name was crossed off the list, Henry, Robert, and Beezus, in their slickers and rain hats, started gathering the soggy papers into bundles and tying them with twine. It was not nearly so much fun as collecting papers.

Mrs. Huggins went to the dime store to buy several balls of twine. When she returned she put on an old raincoat, tied a bandanna over her hair, and joined the boys and Beezus. "I hope we can get these tied up by the Fourth of July," she remarked, and began to stack the soggy papers.

When Mr. Huggins came home from work, he

looked the situation over, changed into an old pair of pants and a mackinaw he usually wore on fishing trips, and went to work. They stacked and tied and stacked and tied. Still the soggy papers stretched ahead of them down the driveway. Henry wished his advertisement had not been so successful.

Mrs. Huggins asked Robert and Beezus to stay for supper, because, she said, if they went home they might not come back. After a hasty meal of string beans, salmon, corn, and applesauce, all out of cans, the five went back to work and tied bundles by the light of a bulb on the back porch. By the time Beezus' and Robert's mothers telephoned to say they had to come home, they had worked their way to the garage. Beezus and Robert did not seem sorry to leave.

Mrs. Huggins sat down on a bundle of papers. "I am too tired to pick up another *Reader's Digest*," she said. "Or even a comic book."

"I think we'd better call it a day," said Mr. Huggins.

Henry sneezed.

"Any idea how you're going to get all these papers to school?" Mr. Huggins asked Friday night, as they knotted the twine on the last bundle.

Henry looked down and kicked at a pile of papers. "We can take some of them in Beezus' wagon and I . . . Well, I sort of thought maybe you'd take some of them in the car."

"Oh, you did," said Mr. Huggins dryly.

On Saturday morning Mr. Huggins and Henry piled both the back seat of the car and the luggage compartment with bundles, which, as Henry found out, were heavier to lift than loose papers and magazines. When the back of the car began to sag, Mr. Huggins said they could not take any more that trip. They drove to Glenwood School, and there they unloaded the car near the auditorium, where the members of the P.T.A. were

measuring bundles and recording the amount brought by each room. Mr. Huggins was not the only father helping out.

The second time Henry and his father loaded the car, the bundles seemed even heavier. Henry looked back at the remaining papers and wondered how many trips they would have to make. Quite a few, he decided. Probably they would have to work all day. He felt tired and his muscles ached. He no longer cared about winning the paper drive. He only wanted to get rid of all that paper.

This time, as Henry and his father unloaded the car, they met Scooter with a bundle of papers he had brought to school in the basket of his bicycle.

"Hi, Scooter," said Henry, because he did not want Scooter to go on being angry with him. "Say . . . there are still a lot of papers in our garage, if you would like a couple of bundles for your room."

"No, thanks," said Scooter coldly.

Well, that's that, thought Henry, disappointed that his peace offering had been rejected. Scooter was mad, and he was going to stay mad. Well, let him, if that was the way he felt. Henry had done his part in trying to make up. It wasn't as though he hoped to fold Scooter's papers again. He was through hanging around.

All day Henry and his father worked, lifting, loading, unloading, stacking, while Mrs. Huggins stayed at school and measured bundles for the P.T.A. Henry was more tired than he had ever been before, but he knew better than to complain. "Maybe we could save some papers for next year's drive," he suggested to his mother, after delivering still another bundle at the school.

"Oh, no, you can't," said Mrs. Huggins promptly, even though she was busy measuring a stack of papers.

Henry stood looking at the piles of paper that

had been collected by the boys and girls of Glenwood School. And more was arriving every minute. He had never before seen so much paper in one place in his whole life. Just about every kind of magazine in the whole United States was piled there. And newspapers! Stacks and stacks of papers. And every one of those papers had been delivered to someone's house by a boy—some other boy.

When Henry and his father had delivered their last bundle to the school yard, and another member of the P.T.A. had relieved Mrs. Huggins of her yardstick, the Huggins family drove wearily home. "I hope our room won," said Henry, without much spirit, "or at least beat old Scooter's room." He decided he was too tired to go back to school later in the afternoon to find out who had won. He could wait until Monday to find out. Right now he did not even want to think about paper.

Monday evening at dinner, Henry, who had

completely recovered from the paper drive, announced to his mother and father, "Well, our room won! I knew we would all the time. We get the six dollars to spend any way we want, except we can't decide how to spend it. And you know what? We beat old Scooter's room by over a thousand inches!"

"And did you get to see the movie?" Mr. Huggins asked.

"We sure did," said Henry. "A cartoon and a nature movie. Of course the movie was pretty educational, but it was good just the same. There was a family of bears in it."

"I worked hard on the paper drive," said Mrs. Huggins. "I would like to see a movie with a family of bears in it too."

Suddenly Henry felt ashamed. Now that he stopped to think about it, his mother and father had worked hard on the paper drive—almost as hard as he had worked. "Thanks for helping," he said, sorry that he had not thanked them sooner. "Even if you didn't get in on the prize." Poor Mom and Dad! They really got the worst of it.

Henry decided that when the next paper drive came around—and that would not be for another year—he would not advertise. That had been too successful. If there happened to be some old papers lying around the house, he would tie them up and take them to school; but right now he felt that he had had enough of paper drives to last a long, long time and he was sure that his mother and father felt the same way. Anyway, next year he hoped somehow, someway, to be too busy doing something *important* to spend a lot of time going around the neighborhood with a wagon and Ramona clonking along behind.

"I guess we'll have to supply our own prize," said Mr. Huggins. "What do you say we stack the dishes and go to the movies? I noticed there was a Western on at the Hollywood, and there might be a family of bears in it."

"Oh, boy!" exclaimed Henry. "Even if it's a school night?"

"Sure," answered Mr. Huggins. "This is a special occasion. We won the paper drive, didn't we?"

CHAPTER FIVE

Henry's New Neighbor

NOT long after the paper drive, a day arrived that Henry had been looking forward to for a long, long time. That day was Henry's eleventh birthday. This year his birthday fell on Saturday, so it was extra-special. Mrs. Huggins invited eight boys from Henry's class for lunch, and Henry received three flashlights (it didn't matter—a boy could always find a use for another flashlight), two packages of stamps to add to his collection, one model airplane kit, and two puzzles. After a lunch of tamales, milk, and a green salad because Mrs. Huggins thought boys should eat vegetables, and an orange ice-cream cake with eleven candles set in whipped cream frosting, the boys entertained themselves by practicing artificial respiration on one another. Then, after Mrs. Huggins had cleared off the table, she drove them to the neighborhood theater, where they saw seventeen Bugs Bunny cartoons, one right after the other.

Henry enjoyed every minute of his birthday. He laughed when Bugs Bunny was Robin Hood, outwitting the Sheriff of Nottingham. He howled when Bugs Bunny escaped from the hunter who wanted to make him into rabbit stew. He shouted when Bugs Bunny switched places with a circus ringmaster who was trying to make him dive off a

high diving board into a bucket of water. And all
the time Henry was thinking, I am eleven years
old now, old enough to have a paper route—if I
could get one.

The boys walked home from the movie, and
when Henry and Robert, who lived near one
another, came to the house the Pumphreys had
lived in, they saw furniture being carried into the
house from a moving van. Naturally they stopped
to watch. Henry was a little disappointed because
the furniture of the new neighbors was not more
interesting. They owned the usual things—beds,
chairs, a stove, a television set.

"Hey, look!" exclaimed Robert, pointing. "A
bike!"

"A boy's bike!" added Henry in excitement. "I
wonder what grade he's in."

"Maybe he'll be in our room," said Robert. "It
was a regular-sized bike."

"You know what would be a good idea?" said

Henry eagerly, as the two boys started toward home. "Maybe the three of us—you and me and this new fellow—could get a bunch of wire and stuff and rig up a telephone system. Of course, to connect it with his house, we would have to string the wires over some fences and through some trees, but I bet it would work."

"Hey, that's a swell idea!" agreed Robert enthusiastically. "We could phone each other any time we wanted to."

"Sure," said Henry. "It would be our own private line. I bet we can find some books at the library that would tell us how to do it."

"I wonder when we will get to meet him," remarked Robert.

"Soon, I hope," answered Henry. "It's going to be fun having a new boy around."

On Sunday Henry found several excuses to ride his bicycle past the new boy's house, but he saw no one. Monday, after school, he noticed curtains at the windows, but still he did not see a boy. When Henry got home he had nothing special to do, so he tied a piece of cellophane to the end of a string and dragged it across the rug for Nosy to pounce on while he wondered what the new boy would be like. Nosy, as Mr. Huggins had predicted, was rapidly growing up to be a cat. Right now he was too big to be a kitten, but still not quite big enough to be a cat. Nosy crouched, lashed his tail, and pounced. With the cellophane in his claws, he rolled over on his back and kicked at his prey with his hind feet, while Ribsy lay watching the game.

The telephone rang and Mrs. Huggins answered it. "Hello?" Henry heard his mother say. "Oh, hello, Eva." Eva, Henry knew, was Scooter's mother. Mrs. McCarthy and Mrs. Huggins often had long, boring conversations over the phone.

"Oh, dear," Henry heard his mother say. "That's too bad."

What's too bad, wondered Henry idly, as he took the cellophane away from Nosy and held it up for the little cat, or big kitten, to jump for.

"I'm glad Henry has been through that already," said Mrs. Huggins.

Now what could I have been through, Henry asked himself, but he could not think of anything he had been through except kindergarten and the first four grades and he did not think his mother and Mrs. McCarthy would be talking about anything like that.

"I wouldn't worry, Eva. It wasn't too bad," said Mrs. Huggins. "But then, of course, Scooter is older."

Maybe Scooter is older than I am, thought Henry, jerking the cellophane free from Nosy's claws, but I am eleven years old now.

"Oh, well, you know how boys are," said Mrs. Huggins.

Henry's interest in the conversation increased. If his mother started talking about how boys were, she might say something he would like to hear. He stopped twirling the cellophane and sat down to listen.

Mrs. Huggins laughed again. "I think that is too funny for words," she said.

Henry became impatient. He hoped it was not something he had done that was too funny for words. He didn't want people laughing at him.

Mrs. Huggins listened for a long time. Finally she said, "I don't know, Eva. I think he's a little young."

Who's a little young for what? Henry was growing more and more impatient. If his mother was talking about his being too young for something, she was probably saying he could not do something he would like to do. Somehow, the things his parents thought he was not old enough to do were always the things he wanted to do most of all. On the chance that his mother was talking about him, Henry went into the kitchen and said in a loud whisper, "I am *not* too young."

Mrs. Huggins motioned him away and went on talking. "But Eva, for one thing, they weigh so much on Sunday."

This baffled Henry. Why wouldn't a thing weigh the same on Sunday as it did on weekdays? His mother's conversation didn't make sense. People certainly did not weigh more on Sunday, unless they ate a lot of apple pie or something. Hey, wait a minute, he thought suddenly. Newspapers! Newspapers weighed more on Sunday! Maybe— no, it couldn't be—yes, it could! His mother must be talking about his delivering papers. No, that couldn't be what she was talking about. Scooter was still mad at him, because of the paper drive.

"Mom," Henry whispered urgently.

Mrs. Huggins put her hand over the mouthpiece

of the telephone. "Henry," she said, "I'm trying to carry on a conversation. Please stop interrupting."

"But Mom—"

Mrs. Huggins gave Henry a look that told him she meant what she said.

"Aw . . ." muttered Henry and went back into the living room, where he picked up Nosy and rubbed the fur on the sides of the kitten's little black face, while he hung on every word his mother said.

"All right, Eva," said Mrs. Huggins at last. "He's been dying to for weeks." But Mrs. Huggins did not hang up. "And by the way, Eva," she went on, "I am in charge of the refreshment committee of the P.T.A. this year and I wondered if you knew of a bakery . . ."

Henry groaned loud enough for his mother to hear, but she paid no attention. ". . . that makes a good inexpensive cake. I thought if we bought a big flat cake and had it iced and decorated with a few rosebuds—oh, no, not a rosebud for every member of the P.T.A.; that would be too expensive—but just enough rosebuds to make it look pretty until we cut it—"

Rosebuds for the P.T.A.! At a time like this! Henry drove his fist into a cushion to work off some of his impatience. When Mrs. Huggins at last ended the conversation, Henry dropped Nosy and sprang to his feet. "What did she want, Mom? What did she want?"

"Henry, when I am talking on the telephone I don't like to be interrupted," said Mrs. Huggins.

"O.K., Mom," agreed Henry hastily. "But what did she want?"

"Scooter has come down with the chicken pox," began Mrs. Huggins.

"Old Scoot has the chicken pox?" exclaimed Henry, as if he could not believe it. "In the seventh grade? Why, I had that when I was a little kid!" Well, what do you know, thought Henry. For once he was ahead of Scooter on something.

"Yes, he has the chicken pox," Mrs. Huggins went on, "and he wants you to take his route until he can go back to school."

"*Scooter* wants *me* to take *his* route?" This was too much for Henry to believe. If his mother had said Mrs. McCarthy had wanted him to take the route, he could believe it—but not Scooter.

"Yes. It seems that he was embarrassed to ask you himself, because of some sort of disagreement you two had." Mrs. Huggins looked amused as she spoke. "And so he asked his mother to phone me about it. He wants you to take his route, because he knows you can do it, but he is afraid you are mad at him."

Maybe Henry had been mad at Scooter, but now that Scooter was sure Henry could do a good job delivering papers, the whole quarrel suddenly seemed unimportant. Just a silly argument a long time ago. "Me? Mad at Scooter?" Henry said, as if he had never heard of such a thing. "When do I start?"

"Today," said his mother. "You'd better go over to Scooter's house and get the route book right now."

Henry had his hand on the doorknob before his mother had finished speaking. "Say, Mom, how long does chicken pox last?" he asked.

"About two weeks, at Scooter's age," answered Mrs. Huggins.

Two weeks! Two whole weeks of delivering papers. And he was eleven years old besides! Henry did not take time to walk down the front steps. He jumped.

The other boys had already begun to fold papers by the time Henry had picked up Scooter's route book and canvas bag and joined them. "Hi," said Henry briefly. "Mr. Capper, I'm taking Scooter's route while he has the chicken pox." Henry found the bundle of papers and began to count them.

"We haven't seen you around for a long time," said Mr. Capper. "Think you can handle it all right?"

"I'm sure I can," answered Henry, and hesitated. "Uh . . . Mr. Capper, I am eleven years old now." Mr. Capper grinned.

"No kidding?" asked Chuck, one of the carriers who went to high school. "Are you really eleven?"

"Sure," boasted Henry. "You didn't think I was going to stay ten all my life, did you?"

"If he's eleven," said Chuck to Mr. Capper, "maybe he could take over my route."

Henry paused in his paper folding long enough to look questioningly at the older boy. "What for?" he asked, suspecting a joke.

"I want to go out for basketball practice in a couple of weeks," explained Chuck.

Satisfied that Chuck was not teasing him, Henry looked expectantly at Mr. Capper, who only smiled and said, "We'll see."

Mr. Capper hadn't made any promises, thought Henry, as he stuffed the last *Journal* into the bag, but he did not think he had anything to worry about. He knew he could handle the route and that Mr. Capper knew he wanted it. Feeling that this time there was nothing to stand in his way, Henry set off to deliver the papers with a light heart.

Henry finished the route by five-thirty and decided to go home by way of the Pumphrey house.
He might catch a glimpse of the new boy. Sure

enough, on the driveway beside the house a
strange boy was unpacking a carton that was filled
with coils of wire, batteries, and what looked like

radio tubes. He was about Henry's age, or maybe a year older—a tall, thin boy, slightly stooped, who wore glasses.

Henry rode part way up the driveway. "Hi," he said, eager to be friendly. "You the new boy?"

"Yup," answered the boy.

Henry felt this did not tell him much. He studied the new boy a moment and decided that he probably was not much of a ball player. That did not matter; there were plenty of boys in the neighborhood who did play ball. "My name is Henry Huggins," Henry said. "I live on the other side of the block, on Klickitat Street."

The boy was so busy untangling some copper wire that he did not bother to answer. Henry felt the conversation was getting no place. This was not the way he had pictured making friends with his new neighbor. Then an old fat dog wandered out of the back yard. He looked something like a fox terrier, only bigger and tougher, as if he might be part bulldog. Henry brightened. Boys always liked to talk about their dogs. "What's your dog's name?" he asked.

"Tiger," answered the boy briefly, as the tired-looking dog flopped down beside him.

"Tiger!" exclaimed Henry. "You can't call a dog Tiger. That's a name for cats."

For the first time the boy put down his wire and looked at Henry through his glasses. "Why?" he asked.

Henry was taken aback. Making friends with this boy was not going to be easy. "Well, I suppose you can," he admitted, because the boy obviously did call his dog Tiger. "What I mean is . . . Well, people usually call dogs Major or Guard or Spot or something like that. What's your name?" Henry asked, both to change the subject and because he wanted to know.

"Byron Murphy," answered the boy. "Call me Murph."

"O.K., Murph," agreed Henry, pleased to have made this much progress in the conversation. He looked at the jumble of wires in Murph's carton and concluded that the new boy must be interested in electricity. And any boy interested in electricity should be glad to help rig up a private telephone line. "Say, Murph," Henry began enthusiastically, "I've got a swell idea. Why don't we get together with my friend Robert, and the three of us rig up our own private telephone line between our houses. We can do it by stringing wires over the fences and through the trees. Then we could talk to each other any time we wanted. We'd have a lot of fun." He looked expectantly at Murph.

Murph went on untangling his wire. "Why couldn't we just telephone each other?" he asked.

Henry stared at Murph as if he could not believe what he had heard. "You—you mean on the regular telephone? The one that belongs to the telephone company?"

"Sure," said Murph.

Henry felt like a balloon with the air let out. "Well, I guess we could," he admitted. Murph was probably right. It would be foolish to buy parts and go to a lot of work and build a telephone system that probably wouldn't work very well, when they already had telephones that did work. But couldn't Murph see that a private telephone system would be *fun?* What kind of a fellow was this Murph?

"Anyway," said Murph, "I'm pretty busy building my robot."

There was one thing about Murph—almost everything he said was a surprise. "You mean you are building a mechanical man?" Henry asked incredulously. By now he was completely bewildered by Murph. Well, he might have expected

something like this. A boy who would name a dog
Tiger would do most anything.

"Sure," said Murph and pulled a five-gallon oil-
can out of the carton. On top of the can was an

old tomato-sauce can which supported a larger
tin can, which Henry could see was supposed to be
the robot's head.

"If you put a funnel upside down on his head, he

would look like the Tin Woodman in *The Wizard of Oz*," offered Henry helpfully. He was beginning to think that this boy had interesting possibilities, even if he was a little peculiar.

"This isn't any Tin Woodman." Murph sounded annoyed. "This is a robot."

Henry felt that Murph thought he wasn't very bright, because he had compared his robot to a character in a fairy tale. "You—you mean you really expect it to work?" he asked cautiously.

"Sure," said Murph. "I've got it all figured out, with batteries and magnets and stuff. I may even put a phonograph inside, so he'll talk."

This was too much for Henry. Murph must be practically a genius. A mechanical man that could talk! There was going to be a lot of excitement in the neighborhood when this news got around. Henry stared at the new boy and his invention until he summoned enough courage to speak again. "What's that hole in his back for?" he asked.

"That's where his insides go," explained Murph.

Henry felt that he should have been able to see that without asking. It was some time before he got up courage to speak again. He did not want to risk any more foolish questions, so he asked, "What are you going to call him?" That should be a good safe question.

"Thorvo," answered Murph.

"That's a good name," agreed Henry, feeling that Thorvo had an interesting outer-space sound appropriate to a robot. He waited hopefully, but Murph seemed too busy to talk. "Well, I guess I better be going," said Henry finally. Then, in one last attempt to be neighborly, he added, "If you ever feel like a game of checkers, I live in that white house around on Klickitat Street."

"Checkers?" repeated Murph absently. "I haven't played checkers for a long time. Not since I learned to play chess."

That settled it as far as Henry was concerned.

Murph was a genius, a real brain. Chess at his age! Everyone knew chess was a game played by wise old men with beards. No wonder he was serious and did not say much. His mind was full of big, important things.

"So long, Murph," said Henry, unable to keep the awe out of his voice. It must be wonderful to be a genius instead of an ordinary checker-playing boy. Murph could probably do anything he wanted to. If he needed something, all he had to do was invent it. And to think that he was going to live right here in the neighborhood!

Henry was sure he had not made a very good impression on Murph with his remarks about Thorvo's looking like the Tin Woodman and his invitation to play an easy game like checkers. He hoped Murph would not think he was too dumb to associate with. Henry was anxious to watch the construction of Thorvo; there had never been anything like Thorvo in the neighborhood in all the time he could remember. He searched for something to say that would show Murph he wasn't so dumb after all. "I'll see you around," he finally said. "I'm pretty busy after school, delivering papers." That ought to show Murph he wasn't so dumb. A boy with a paper route was pretty important.

"A route takes a lot of time," agreed Murph, showing more interest than he had in anything Henry had said so far.

"I'm substituting for a couple of weeks," said Henry, glad of the opportunity to talk about his work for a change. "Then one of the carriers is quitting, and I expect I'll get his route."

Instantly Henry was sorry he had spoken. Maybe this new boy was looking for a route too. "Well, so long," he said hastily, and coasted down the driveway.

Now I've gone and done it, thought Henry, as he rode home. Here he practically had a route of his own, and then he had to go and let this new boy, this brain, know that a carrier was giving up his route. How dumb can I get? Henry asked himself in disgust. Now Murph would probably go after the route, and what chance did Henry have against a brain who went around playing chess and inventing a robot named Thorvo? Not a chance, Henry decided. Not a chance at all. Murph would probably not only get the route, he would build a mechanical man to deliver the papers for him.

CHAPTER SIX

Ramona Takes Over

NEWS of Byron Murphy, genius, quickly spread throughout the neighborhood. All the boys and girls for blocks around walked, roller-skated, or bicycled past Murph's house several times a day, hoping to catch a glimpse of the new boy and his mechanical man. If they saw him working in the garage they gathered on the driveway a respectful distance away, to watch. As arms made out of pipes were added to the tin body, and the tin-can head was topped with an antenna, some were sure the robot would work when Murph finished it. Others scoffed at the whole idea.

There was one member of the neighborhood who did not stay a respectful distance from Murph. That was Ramona. She was not one bit awed by a genius. Clonking in her high-heeled shoes, she tagged around the garage after him. Of all the boys and girls, she was the only one who thought Tiger was a good name for a dog. She said that if she ever had a dog she was going to name it Tiger, after Murph's dog. Murph ignored Ramona, but this did not bother her at all.

Henry could see that Beezus was ashamed to have a little sister who was such a nuisance to a genius at work. He felt like telling Ramona not to be such a pest, but he decided he had better

keep still. He was as eager as the others to watch the progress of Thorvo, but at the same time he did not want to call attention to himself and perhaps start Murph thinking about a paper route.

Then one afternoon, when Henry had finished delivering Scooter's papers, he went to the barbershop for a haircut. On the way home he saw Murph riding toward him on a bicycle, with Tiger puffing along half a block behind. Over Murph's shoulders Henry was astonished to see an empty *Journal* bag. At the sight of that bag, Henry suddenly felt more cheerful than he had felt since Murph had moved into the neighborhood.

"Hi there, Murph," Henry called out, with sudden enthusiasm. "I didn't know you had a paper route. I've never seen you around Mr. Capper's garage with the rest of the fellows."

"My route is in my old neighborhood," Murph explained.

"Oh," was all Henry said, because he was busy thinking that he no longer had to worry about having a genius take a paper route away from him. Now he and Murph could be friends. Maybe Murph would even let him help work on Thorvo— not doing the hard parts, that took a lot of brains, but things like handing him wrenches and tightening screws. He could probably save Murph plenty of time. Henry Huggins, assistant to a genius—that's what he would be.

And so on Saturday, when all the boys and girls in the neighborhood except Scooter—who was still confined to his house with chicken pox—gathered at Murph's garage to watch the progress of Thorvo, Henry no longer felt that he had to be quiet. "What are you going to make his legs out of?" Henry asked.

"Pipe," answered Murph. "Thick pipe, when I can find some."

"Maybe I can find some for you," said Henry eagerly.

"If you put a funnel on him for a hat, he would look like the Tin—" one of the girls started to suggest.

Henry interrupted to keep her from annoying Murph with what she was about to say. "There's a plumber over by the supermarket," he said quickly. "He might have some pieces of pipe you could have."

Murph did not answer; he was too busy hunting for something in a box.

Beezus and Ramona came running up the driveway to join the rest of Murph's audience. This time Ramona was not clonking along in high-heeled shoes. Instead, she had perched on her nose the frames of a pair of old sunglasses. They were much too big for her, and to keep them from falling off,

the sidepieces were tied together at the back of her head with a piece of string.

I sure am glad she's not my sister, thought Henry.

"I'm wearing glasses, like Murph," announced Ramona happily.

"She kept asking and asking for a pair of glasses so she would look like Murph," Beezus explained apologetically, "until Mother finally found an old pair and took the glass out for her."

Murph paid no attention to his admirer. He found part of a string of old Christmas-tree lights and fitted two of them into sockets in the robot's head.

"Are his eyes going to light up?" asked Robert, with a touch of awe in his voice.

"Of course," answered Murph.

"Oh, Murph!" exclaimed Beezus. "You can put in blue Christmas-tree bulbs, and he'll have blue eyes!"

"Thorvo's eyes are going to be red," stated Murph definitely.

Beezus looked embarrassed, as if she should have realized how silly she was to think a robot should have blue eyes.

"I think red eyes are pretty," said Ramona, moving closer to Murph. As she stood by his elbow she began to practice whistling. She puckered up her mouth and blew, but no whistle came out. Then she tried sucking in through her puckered lips and succeeded in producing a hollow whistling sound, as if she were blowing across the mouth of a bottle. It was not a pleasant sound, but she liked it, and she repeated it over and over.

"Sh-h, Ramona!" whispered Beezus. "You might bother Murph."

"Yes," agreed Henry, not wanting to see genius disturbed. "You better keep quiet."

But Ramona went right on with her whistling.

Between delivering Scooter's papers and watching Murph's progress on Thorvo, Henry found that time passed quickly. Finally the day arrived when Scooter was able to take over his route once more. On that day Henry went along with Scooter, who was once more his friend, to Mr. Capper's garage. "Say, Mr. Capper," he said, satisfied that he had done a good job on Scooter's route, "I do get to take Chuck's route, don't I?"

Mr. Capper looked sympathetic—so sympathetic that Henry braced himself for a terrible disappointment. "Well, Henry, I'm afraid not," Mr. Capper said kindly.

"You—you mean I don't get the route after all?" stammered Henry, hoping that he had not understood Mr. Capper.

"I'm sorry, Henry," answered Mr. Capper.

Miserable with disappointment, Henry stared at Mr. Capper. He was too overcome to say anything. He had been so sure, even though Mr.

Capper had not made any promises, that this time he was going to get the route.

"Aw, Mr. Capper," protested Scooter.

Henry felt encouraged at having Scooter stand up for him, instead of scoffing, as he usually did. "I—I thought you needed someone to take Chuck's route," he ventured.

"I did," answered Mr. Capper. "But one of the other district managers phoned me about a boy in his district who wanted to shift to this neighborhood."

"Oh," said Henry miserably. So that was why some other boy was going to have the route. It was not anything that he had done wrong. All the same, Henry felt embarrassed. Everyone who knew how much he wanted a route would think it was pretty funny when someone else started delivering *Journals*. Everyone would think Mr. Capper didn't want him to have the route.

Henry felt especially embarrassed to have the other carriers see his humiliation. If only he had come early and talked to Mr. Capper alone. Henry kicked miserably at the bag Scooter was filling with *Journals*.

All at once a terrible suspicion leaped into Henry's mind. "Say, Mr. Capper, would you mind telling me the name of the new carrier?" he asked.

"Let's see." Mr. Capper frowned thoughtfully. "It was Bryan—no, that wasn't it."

"Byron Murphy?" prompted Henry.

"Yes. Yes, that's the name," agreed Mr. Capper.

So it was Murph, thought Henry bitterly. And after I offered to help him find some pipe for his robot's legs, too. A fine friend he turned out to be!

"Is he someone you know?" Mr. Capper asked.

"Sort of," muttered Henry. Well, Murph had the route and he did not, and there was nothing Henry could do about it. That in itself was enough to make him want to avoid the new boy. It wasn't that Henry had done anything wrong; it was just that Murph had experience, and a district manager to speak for him. Naturally, thought Henry. A genius can do anything, anything at all.

After that Henry wished Murph had not moved into the neighborhood. The old genius, Henry thought crossly. It did not seem fair for Murph to have a paper route and be a genius, too. Every afternoon when Murph finished his route, Henry saw him ride down Klickitat Street with the empty *Journal* bag over his shoulders and Tiger puffing along behind. This made Henry feel worse. Once he rode past Murph's house and yelled, "I hope your old robot doesn't work!" No one heard him, but he felt better for having relieved his feelings.

Then one day when Henry was returning from a swim at the Y., he turned a corner near Beezus' house and saw Ramona, with her arms full of *Journals*, skipping along the sidewalk. Murph was nowhere in sight.

That's funny, thought Henry.

"Hey!" yelled Murph, appearing around the corner on his bicycle. "You come back with my papers!" When Ramona ran on down the street, Murph pursued her.

Well, what do you know, thought Henry, as he stopped his bicycle and sat with one foot against the curb to watch this interesting scene.

When Murph caught up with Ramona, he jumped off his bicycle and yelled, "You give me those papers!"

"No!" shrieked Ramona. "I want to deliver them. I'm a paper boy!"

Murph grabbed the papers. Ramona hung on and screamed. Faces began to appear in windows. Front doors opened, and the neighbors stepped outside to see what was happening. Tiger arrived on the scene, but he only lay down on the sidewalk and looked tired.

Henry rode a little closer to have a better view

of the struggle. He could see that Murph was
pretty embarrassed to have the whole neighborhood watch him tussling with a four-year-old with
empty sunglass frames tied around her head. He

did look pretty foolish—not a bit like a genius.

Murph jerked the papers away from Ramona. Kicking and howling, she threw herself on the sidewalk. "You give me back my papers!" she screamed.

"They aren't your papers," said Murph, his face and ears so crimson with embarrassment that Henry almost felt sorry for him, because he knew how exasperating Ramona could be. This time Murph did not yell, because he was trying to look dignified in front of the neighbors.

When Ramona beat her fists on the sidewalk, Henry could not help grinning. He could see that she was working up to a really good tantrum and that Murph, who was not used to her tantrums, wished he was a million miles away.

Then Beezus came running around the corner. "Ramona Quimby!" she said sternly. "You know you aren't supposed to run off! Get up this very instant!"

Ramona screamed and kicked her heels on the cement, exactly the way Henry knew she would. "I'm sorry, Murph," Beezus apologized. "I don't know how she got away."

Murph looked a little scared, as if somehow he were to blame for the scene. Hunching his shoulders as if he hoped to become invisible, Murph climbed on his bicycle with the papers, while Beezus grabbed her sister by the hand and tried to drag her to her feet. Ramona went so limp that she appeared to have no more bones than a rag doll. Beezus put her hands under Ramona's arms and started dragging her toward home. Wearily Tiger rose to his feet and trotted after Murph.

When the girls were far enough away so that he would not have to speak to Murph, Henry rode up to Beezus. "Hi," he said, above Ramona's howls. "Need any help?"

"I don't know what would do any good," said Beezus, and Ramona stopped howling to listen.

"Ramona insists she is going to deliver papers."

"I'm a paper boy," said Ramona. "I have to deliver papers."

"You keep quiet," snapped Beezus.

"She sure gave old Murph a bad time," said Henry, trying not to show how entertained he had been.

Beezus sighed. "You know how Ramona is when she gets to pretending."

"I know," answered Henry, remembering the trouble he had had with Ramona during the paper drive, when she pretended she was a monkey. Oh, well, thought Henry, Murph will figure out a way to handle Ramona. Murph could do anything. That was the handy thing about being a genius.

The days that followed were difficult ones for Henry. He played with Nosy, brushed Ribsy, went swimming at the Y.—all the things he usually did —but something was wrong. Somehow he could not get interested in anything. If he were smart like Murph, he could invent a robot of his own to keep him busy, but the trouble was, he was not smart like Murph.

Then one afternoon when Henry was putting his bicycle in the garage, he was surprised to see Murph, with the empty *Journal* bag over his shoulders, riding up the driveway toward him. Now what can he want, Henry wondered, and cautiously decided to let Murph have the first word.

Murph came to the point at once. "You can have the route," he said.

Henry was too surprised to speak.

Murph looked extremely uncomfortable. "I said you can have the route," he repeated.

"You mean you don't want it?" Henry asked incredulously.

"Nope," said Murph, as Tiger caught up with him and collapsed on the driveway, panting.

"How come?" asked Henry, finding it hard to believe that a boy who had a paper route would be willing to give it up.

"Ramona," answered Murph.

"Ramona!" exclaimed Henry in disbelief. "She's just a little kid!" A genius licked by a four-year-old! If he hadn't been so surprised, Henry would have laughed out loud.

"I know," said Murph miserably, "but she sure can make a lot of trouble."

To keep from answering, Henry pretended to find something wrong with the chain on his bicycle. He wanted the route, all right. He had wanted it for weeks, and no matter how much trouble Ramona caused Murph, Henry did not intend to let any four-year-old girl stand in his way. It was not the thought of Ramona that kept him from answering. It was Mr. Capper. Henry was not sure the district manager would let him have the route.

Murph must have guessed what Henry was thinking, because he looked down at the driveway and said, "It's all right with Mr. Capper." Murph hesitated before he went on. "I asked him, and he said he would be glad to have you take the route."

The route is mine, thought Henry in a daze. Mr. Capper said so.

Murph looked thoroughly miserable as he continued. "I guess I shouldn't have taken the route when I knew you wanted it, but I just had to have it. Dad said my other route was too far away from home. I needed money to buy parts for Thorvo. Dad thinks Thorvo is a waste of time, so I have to earn the money for parts myself and . . . well, I just had to have the route. But I've been having so much trouble I probably would have lost the route, and anyway, I don't want it. It takes all my time trying to straighten things out, and I don't have any time left to work on Thorvo. . . ."

Murph's voice trailed away, and he looked unhappily at Henry through his glasses.

Henry found himself feeling sorry for Murph, whether he wanted to or not. It must be hard to have a father who thought building a robot was a waste of time, and to have to wear glasses, and not to be a good ballplayer. Why, Murph didn't even have a good dog like Ribsy. He only had tired old Tiger. And then Henry realized the importance of what Murph had said. The route was really his. "Sure, Murph," he managed to say at last. "I'll take the route."

"Swell." Murph was visibly relieved. He removed the *Journal* bag, pulled the route book out of his hip pocket, and handed both to Henry. Then he began to speak eagerly, as if he wanted to make up for what he had done. "I'll have to put Thorvo away for a while until I figure out how to earn some money for parts, and if you still want to go ahead with that private telephone I have most of the stuff we would need. And we wouldn't even have to go to the library to find out how to do it, because I already know how to build one."

"You do!" exclaimed Henry. "Hey, that's swell!" A genius was going to be a pretty good person to have around the neighborhood after all.

"Maybe we can get started Saturday," said Murph, as he started to leave. "You'll be pretty busy with the route after school."

"That's right. My route will take up a lot of my time," agreed Henry. "So long. See you Saturday." Stunned by his sudden good fortune, Henry continued to stand on the driveway in a daze. He had a paper route, and all because of Ramona, but somehow he could not quite believe it. In spite of the bag and the route book in his hands, his good luck did not seem real.

The next day at school, in order to convince himself that his route was real, Henry mentioned it every time he got a chance. When school was finally out, he went straight to Mr. Capper's garage, where he enjoyed being one of the gang at last. Even more he enjoyed starting out with the heavy bag of papers over his shoulders. The route was real, all right.

Henry had not gone far, however, when he saw something that made him pause. Ramona was sitting on the curb, with her feet in the gutter and her hands folded in her lap. She was no longer wearing the sunglasses, and Beezus was nowhere in sight. "Hello there, Ramona," said Henry. In a roundabout way he had her to thank for the route.

"Hello, Henry," said Ramona demurely.

I don't see what Murph was so bothered about,

Henry told himself, and went on delivering papers. Ramona continued to sit on the curb like a good girl. She just wants to watch, thought Henry, feeling grown-up and businesslike. Since she wasn't wearing her sunglass frames, she had probably forgotten all about pretending she was a paper boy. He grinned at the thought of Murph's being intimidated by a little girl who sat on the curb with her hands folded in her lap.

Cheerfully Henry rode into the next street, but as he tossed papers he began to have an uneasy feeling that something was wrong. Ramona had been too good. It was not natural. She must be up to something.

Just to be on the safe side, Henry circled the block so that he was riding up Ramona's street once more. And there was Ramona skipping along the sidewalk, with her arms full of the papers he had just delivered. She was tossing them wherever she felt like letting them fall.

That Ramona! I might have known, Henry told himself. "Hey, cut that out!" he yelled furiously.

Ramona tossed a paper onto a lawn—the wrong lawn. Henry took off after her. When he reached her he let his bicycle fall to the sidewalk while he grabbed at the papers Ramona was clutching. "You give me those," Henry said fiercely.

"No!" screamed Ramona. "I'm going to deliver them!"

Henry knew what was going to happen next. He had seen it all before, only the first time he had thought it funny. Where was Beezus, anyway? She might know what to do. Henry jerked the papers away from Ramona, who threw herself on the sidewalk exactly as he had expected. This is where I came in, thought Henry grimly.

Ramona shrieked and grabbed his ankle with both hands. Henry tried to shake her loose, but she hung on.

"Beezus!" Henry yelled. "Beezus, come here!"

Faces began to appear at the windows, and Henry felt extremely foolish and not at all businesslike to be standing there yelling for a girl to come and help him. Ribsy, who had been left at home so that he would not get into fights with dogs along the route, came running down the street at the sound of Henry's voice.

Beezus ran out of her house. "Ramona Geraldine Quimby!" She sounded completely exasperated. "You're supposed to be in the house. You know Mother said you had to stay in your room."

Ribsy barked furiously.

"I'm a paper boy," said Ramona stubbornly.

"Get her off my ankle, will you?" said Henry. Tackled by a four-year-old, with the whole neighborhood watching! Henry felt a flash of sympathy for Murph.

Ribsy grabbed Ramona's coveralls in his teeth. There was a sound of tearing cloth. Ramona screamed.

"Ribsy, cut that out!" Henry ordered. Now people would probably think Ribsy was a ferocious dog attacking Ramona, and there was no telling what trouble that could lead to.

Beezus pried Ramona's fingers from Henry's

ankle and started dragging her sister toward home.

"Quiet, Ribsy!" Henry said to his barking dog. "It's all right, fellow. She wasn't really hurting me."

"I'm sorry, Henry," Beezus apologized above her sister's howls. "I don't know what we can do. (Ramona, be *quiet!*) Mother says she has to stay in her room until the papers are delivered, but if she doesn't get out one day, she gets out the next."

"We've got to do something," said Henry desperately. "I can't have people phoning complaints about not getting their papers all the time. I'll lose my route. Can't you think of something?"

"I've tried," answered Beezus. "The trouble is, when Ramona knows we don't want her to do something, that just makes her want to do it all the more. Mother says she is just plain contrary."

"Yeah, I know," said Henry gloomily as he looked at Ramona, who had stopped screaming and was listening with interest. Suddenly the sight of Ramona looking so pleased to be the center of attention made Henry angry. Who did she think she was, anyway? She wasn't so important. She was just a girl who went to nursery school and played in a sand pile; that was all. She wasn't going to get him into trouble. He was eleven years old and she was only four. If he couldn't figure out a way to keep her from bothering him, he wasn't very smart. Maybe he wasn't a genius, but he was still smarter than a four-year-old. If she continued her game, and of course she would unless he did something about it, he would get into as much trouble as Murph had. And Henry had no intention of going to Mr. Capper the first thing and saying he couldn't deliver the papers because of a girl who went to nursery school. No, sir!

Henry glared at Ramona and thought hard. The thing to do was to outwit her. But how? He had done it once when she had pretended she was a monkey and he would have to do it again. He could get some old papers and fold them and let her deliver them. No, that wouldn't work. People would pick them up and think he had delivered old papers. Somehow, he had to keep her from pretending she was a paper boy. He could . . . What *could* he do? And all at once Henry had an inspiration. If only he had enough time. . . .

Henry looked at his watch. The papers did not have to be delivered until six o'clock. That would give him just about half an hour to see if his idea would work before he finished his route. All he needed was a box, some wire, a pair of scissors, and some red paint—no, his mother's lipstick would be quicker—and a few other things.

"Beezus, you hang onto Ramona," he directed. "I'll be back in half an hour. No matter what happens, don't let her get away."

Ramona looked fascinated. She could hardly wait to see what was going to happen.

"Henry, what are you going to do?" Beezus called after him.

"You'll see," answered Henry mysteriously. "Come on, Ribsy!"

Henry rode home as fast as he could, and when he got there he worked fast. He had to, if he was going to finish his idea in time to deliver his papers. Scraps of cardboard and bits of Scotch tape fell to the floor, but Henry did not bother to pick them up. There wasn't time. At last, and not a moment too soon, his creation was finished.

Henry's creation consisted of a cardboard hatbox with a wire coat hanger fastened upside down to the top. In one side of the box he had cut holes for eyes and a mouth. These he had outlined with lipstick, because Ramona said she liked red eyes. Henry set the hatbox over his head and looked into the mirror. Not bad, he thought, not bad at all. Really gruesome. Of course it was pretty crude, but a girl who could pretend that a jumping rope was a monkey's tail would not be too particular.

"Goodness, Henry!" exclaimed Mrs. Huggins, as Henry dashed through the living room. "You scared me!"

Henry did not stop to talk. He rode as fast as he could to the Quimbys' house, where Beezus and Ramona were waiting on the front steps.

"Henry!" exclaimed Beezus, when she saw his cardboard head. "Are you getting ready for Halloween?"

"Nope," said Henry, as he lifted off his head and held it out to Ramona. "How would you like to be a mechanical man like Thorvo?" he asked, and held his breath as he waited to see if Ramona liked his suggestion.

Ramona beamed. There was nothing she liked better than pretending.

Henry relaxed and set the head on her shoulders. "Now remember," he cautioned. "A mechanical man can't move very fast, and he jerks along

when he walks." That was to keep her from getting
any ideas about being a robot who delivered
papers.

"Clank, clank," answered Ramona, jerking
down the steps.

"A mechanical man can't bend at the waist,
because he doesn't have any," Henry added.

"Clank," answered Ramona.

Henry and Beezus exchanged a look of relief. His route was safe! Henry could see that Beezus was impressed with his idea. And it was pretty smart of him to think of it, Henry thought modestly. Maybe he wasn't a genius like Murph, but he wasn't so dumb, either. In some ways he was even smarter than Murph. Henry found himself pleased with the thought of being smarter than a genius.

"Henry, what a wonderful idea!" Beezus sounded truly grateful. "Now she will be lots easier to chase."

Henry grinned. "Well, so long," he said, and mounted his bicycle. "I've got to get on with my route." *His route*. Henry felt like shouting the words so the whole world could hear them, because at last he was doing what he wanted to do—something important. And on Saturday he and Murph would start building their own private telephone line. Good old Murph! It was lucky he had moved into the neighborhood. Life, Henry discovered,

was suddenly so full of interesting things to do
that he rode his bicycle through a pile of autumn
leaves in the gutter just for the joy of hearing them
crackle.

"Clank, clank!" Ramona yelled after him.

"Clank, clank!" answered Henry.